The Hope

The Rebekah Series: Book Three

JENIFER JENNINGS

Peacock Press
3040 Plantation Ridge Drive
Green Cove Springs, FL 32043

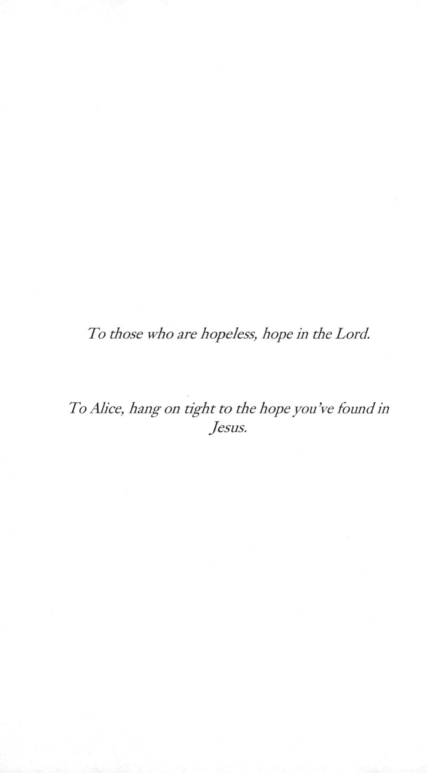

To those who are hopeless, hope in the Lord.

To Alice, hang on tight to the hope you've found in Jesus.

Chapter 1

"The children struggled together within her, and she said, 'If it is thus, why is this happening to me?'…"
-Genesis 25:22

Beerlahairoi, 2005 B.C.
Rebekah

Rebekah tried to lean over her expanded belly to reach

the dough that sat in a shallow bowl between her feet. Her fingers barely pressed into the soft ball.

The baby in her womb displayed displeasure at being adjusted with a swift kick to her insides.

"Ow!" She rubbed her stomach.

"Here," Hadiya pulled the bowl close to herself and pressed her fingers into the pliable mound, "let me do that. You need your rest."

Rebekah rolled her eyes at her handmaid. "All I do is rest."

"And look how well it has given your little one a chance to thrive."

Rebekah rubbed the top of her ever-growing midsection. "Yes, well, this little one better stop thriving or soon there will be no more room left."

Hadiya chuckled softly while she kneaded the dough.

"How much longer will I have to endure this misery?"

"Misery, is it now?" The handmaiden's eyes never left her task. "You did nothing but yearn for your womb to be open for twenty harvest cycles and now that Elohim has answered your many prayers suddenly His blessing is a curse?"

Rebekah flinched. As much as she didn't want to admit it, Hadiya was right. "I didn't mean it like that. I'm just so…"

"Uncomfortable. I know." She shook her head. "You've wanted so much to be like Eve, but you forgot her deception brought this particular part of the experience upon all mothers."

"Why did I ever pray to—" Another blow to her inside confirmed Hadiya's point. Rebekah attempted to adjust herself near the fire, but it seemed no position soothed the baby-to-come. She looked helplessly at her handmaid. "Is there anything that can be done?"

"We can inquire of the other women and see if any of them have ever experienced such."

"You're wise beyond your years." She flinched at another painful internal punch.

Hadiya stood and dusted flour from her hands. "I'll start now and find Deborah to help finish up these loaves."

Rebekah bit down on her bottom lip. "Hurry," she grunted through clenched teeth.

Hadiya rushed toward the nearest tent.

Rebekah tried to reach the kneading bowl, but each movement seemed to gain more protests from her unborn child. A few more blows frustrated her attempts enough to give up and try to stand. She carefully rolled to her hands and knees. Her first efforts were met with internal objections.

A familiar, calloused hand cradled her elbow. "You should wait for help."

Rebekah looked up into the cloudy eyes of her nurse, Deborah. "Did Hadiya find you?"

She nodded and set her feet to help with Rebekah's weight. "She mentioned you were having a rough morning."

"Rough doesn't begin to—" She grabbed her aching stomach. "Ow!"

"Let's get you into your tent."

"I want to walk around a bit," she panted through short breaths. "The baby seems a little calmer when I'm moving." She leaned on Deborah until she was on her swollen feet. With shuffling steps, Rebekah lapped her cooking fire.

Deborah kept her hands on Rebekah's elbow trying to bear some of her weight.

Hadiya returned with a few women trailing behind her. "These are the most experienced mothers I could find."

Rebekah nodded to the group. "Ladies, any help you could offer would be greatly appr—" Pain sent her doubled over, forcing her hands to her knees.

"Labor?" One woman stepped forward and placed a hand on the top of Rebekah's stomach.

"Can't be," another argued. "She still has at least another two moon cycles to go before the baby is due."

"But look at her," a third protested. "Maybe her count is off."

"Not labor." The first shook her head. "The top of her stomach is soft."

"Maybe false labor?" the second suggested.

"Possible." The first woman rubbed her pointed chin. "Though I've never seen even false labor come on this strong."

Deborah rubbed Rebekah's lower back. "Can you think of anything at all that might explain this?"

The women stood silently filtering through their combined years of birthing babies.

"What is going on here?" A recognizable voice, though strained with concern, called behind the group.

Rebekah looked up to find Eliezer rushing to her side. She reached for him, still unable to straighten to her full height.

He grabbed her hand and shifted her weight to his aged frame. "Mistress Rebekah, you look as white as spun wool. Are you ill?"

She shook her head and pointed to her stomach with her free hand.

His eyes darted to her midsection. "Has your labor begun?"

"We don't think so," the first woman with the pointed chin answered. "To be honest, none of us know what is happening to her."

"Has anyone called Master Isaac from the fields?"

The women exchanged uncertain glances.

"Go then. Tell him his wife needs him."

Two of the women picked up the hems of their dresses and headed in the direction the shepherds had set out for only hours before.

"Now, you two," Eliezer turned to Deborah and Hadiya, "get the Mistress some fresh water and make sure she has a comfortable spot in her tent. I'll escort her in."

"I'm well—" Rebekah tried to speak, but the pain overtook her words again.

He snorted. "If you're fine, then I am a bright-eyed boy."

She chuckled despite her agony. No matter how old Abraham's most trusted servant got, his eyes still reminded her of a handsome youth he must have been so long ago.

"Come," his tone took on that of a decisive leader, "I'm taking you into your tent to rest. When Master Isaac gets here, we shall figure this out together."

Rebekah wanted to protest further, but the increased pain in her midsection stole her strength along with her arguments. Perhaps a rest would do her some good. She yielded to his gentle leading.

Eliezer turned her toward her tent and helped ease her onto a reed-mat Hadiya had laid out in the open area along with as many soft skins as she could find. "There now, just rest. Your husband should be along shortly."

Rebekah closed her eyes.

Rebekah didn't know how long she had been asleep, but the sound of Isaac's voice woke her. She opened her eyes to find him sitting on one side of her while Eliezer sat on the other.

A hint of teasing played at Isaac's lips and his eyes

were soft toward her. "I thought I told you to take it easy."

"I didn't make it through one dough ball before your child decided to protest," her voice croaked through a parched throat.

Eliezer slid his hand under her head to raise it slightly and lifted a cup to her lips. "Drink."

She parted her lips and took in the cool water, draining the cup.

"Now," Isaac adjusted his legs, "tell me what has brought me from the fields."

Rebekah shook her head. "I'm not sure. I've been in such terrible pain lately."

"Pain is a natural part of childbearing."

Her attention drifted toward the fluttering tent flap. "The other women think it odd as well. I think this is something different."

"I see."

Rebekah turned to look him in the eyes, but his focus had shifted toward the servant. She licked her lips. "Is there a way to…I mean…Abraham can…"

Both men stared at her with concern etched on their faces.

She dropped her gaze. "Can we ask Elohim?"

Isaac glared at Eliezer.

The servant's eyes darted to the ceiling and back again.

She scrunched her brow. She knew the old man well enough to read him like a scroll. "So, there is a way?"

Isaac shook his head. "I know *Abba* hears Elohim, but it is usually Elohim who speaks to *Abba*, not the other way around."

Eliezer closed his eyes and let out a long breath.

"Eliezer?" Rebekah whispered his name.

He turned his attention to her. His eyes were bright and kind.

"Do you know something?"

He gave a short nod.

"Tell me."

"There is another who might be willing to hear such a matter and would be able to entreat Elohim for you."

Isaac leaned over Rebekah. "Who?"

"Melchizedek." Eliezer's focus moved to Rebekah's midsection. "He is Priest-King of Salem. Abraham encountered him on our travels. He is said to be very wise and seeks Elohim on matters such as this." His gaze shifted to Rebekah's. "It's a slim chance."

"At this point, I'll take any." As if to confirm her words, a kick came from inside her womb.

"But Salem is far." Isaac shook his head. "And I can't leave at this time in the season."

Eliezer bowed his head. "I will be honored to escort Mistress Rebekah."

"That's thoughtful of you, but should she really be traveling this close to her time?"

Eliezer looked to Rebekah.

"I'm strong." She smiled. "Elohim will be with me."

Isaac curled inward. "I guess that settles the matter." He straightened. "By the way, Eliezer, what brought you to Beerlahairoi to begin with?"

He smiled and looked up to the ceiling. "As a matter of fact, Abraham sent me to check on Rebekah since he had received no news of her progress."

Isaac rubbed the back of his neck. "I guess I'm not very good at sending messages to *Abba*." He spread his hands in front of himself. "Life seems to be moving faster than I'd like most days."

"That it does, Master Isaac, that it does."

"Speaking of which," Isaac stood, "I've got to get back to the fields." He looked down at his heavily pregnant wife. "Are you sure about this trip?"

"I know I'm in good hands." She reached over and squeezed Eliezer's hand.

"Very well. I'll leave word with the servants to prepare anything you request, Eliezer." He moved to the door, but hesitated. "Please, just bring her back safely."

Eliezer chuckled. "If I managed to bring her all the way from Padanaram, I think we can manage a trip to Salem and back."

Pain flashed in Isaac's eyes. "But as I recall, it wasn't an event-free journey."

"You can trust me, Master Isaac." Eliezer didn't show any sign of the painful truth hitting its mark. "I will guard your treasure with my very life." He squeezed Rebekah's hand.

Isaac's demeanor eased. "I know you will." He turned and headed out of the tent.

Rebekah sat up. "Well, if we are serious about heading out as soon as possible, we'd better start preparing."

"You rest." He put a gentle hand on her shoulder. "I will make all the arrangements."

She sighed. "At least send in Hadiya. I'm sure she's not going to let me out of her sight."

Chapter 2

"…So she went to inquire of the LORD."
-Genesis 25:22

Salem

Seven days later, Rebekah gave praise to Elohim when she saw the city of Salem come into view in the distance. The days had been long for Rebekah atop a camel with a still-growing child inside her who seemed to object to the ride as much as her aching body.

Hadiya, who had insisted on accompanying her, filled the days with excited chatter about all Rebekah's hopes and dreams for the little-one-to-come.

Rebekah glanced over her shoulder to her handmaiden who rode on the camel behind her. A noticeable wave of relief washed over her as she spotted the city as well.

Eliezer pushed the lead camel toward the impressive city that stood before them.

Salem, like many Canaanite cities, was heavily

fortressed and built on top of a hill. Its stone walls and well-designed layout impressed any visitor who was privileged to enter its gates.

Rebekah eyed the many buildings they passed as they traveled the main street. "How are we going to find Melchizedek?"

"Well," Eliezer pulled at his long beard, "he is both priest and king. I would assume we could either find him in the temple or the palace." He looked up at her. "Knowing the little I know about the man, I say we try the temple first."

Hadiya leaned over her camel. "Do you know which way that is?"

The old servant looked up one street and down another. "No." He smiled up at her. "But this city is no different than any other. If we can find the market street, we can find someone willing to point us in the right direction."

"And how do we find the market in a city where we've never been?"

He put his finger on his nose and gave the woman a quick wink. "Just follow the smell."

Rebekah shook her head as a smirk spread across her face. She silently thanked Elohim for giving her a wise guide.

It wasn't long before the scents of a bustling market reached them; then the sights. Animals and people moved all around.

Eliezer found an idol maker carving away and

inquired of the man. "Could you please point us in the direction of the temple?"

The seller sneered. "Which one?"

"The one in which we can find King Melchizedek."

"Oh, that one." He pointed north. "Follow this street here until it ends. You'll see the building. Can't miss it."

"Thank you." Eliezer bowed and turned the camel's reins in the direction the man indicated.

The sway of the camel suddenly turned Rebekah's stomach. "I'll be glad to dismount."

Hadiya huffed. "I'll be glad when we get you back to your tent."

"This is the most excitement I've had in a while." Rebekah took in a deep breath. "I'm enjoying it."

The trio made their way through the crowded streets until the road under their feet ended. A group of buildings stood before them. One higher than the rest and immaculately well maintained. An inscription near the door announced to all who passed, "Temple of the Most High God."

"I think we found it." Eliezer inspected the inscription. "Let's hope Melchizedek is here." He signaled for the camels to kneel and helped the women down. Once they were off, he ordered the camels to stand again and found a post nearby to tie their leads to.

Rebekah rubbed at her stomach. Since the movement ceased her pains had started again.

"This way." Eliezer held out his arm for her to lean on.

She appreciated the support, but felt guilty for having to use the limited strength of the older man.

The three passed through the door and found themselves in the open courtyard of a busy temple. People rushed here and there. Most dressed in fine linens assisting the commoners who entered.

Eliezer stopped one of them. "Excuse me, but we would like to see King Melchizedek."

The man let out a short snort. "You and half the city, traveler." He looked the three of them up and down. "You can leave your offerings with one of the temple servants."

"We're not here to leave an offering; we need to see the king," he demanded.

"The king is a very busy man."

Eliezer took in a deep breath.

Rebekah knew that look. The faithful servant was making a silent request to a higher authority than the priest standing before him or even the king who sat on the throne in Salem. She smiled.

"I can appreciate how busy the king is," Eliezer said in a calm voice, "but if you would just get a message to him, I'm sure he would see us."

Obvious doubt crossed the man's face. He adjusted his weight as he thought. "One name, but that's it. I'm not a messenger."

"Tell King Melchizedek that Abram's servant,

Eliezer is requesting to see him."

"Abram's servant." He looked at both women.

"Yes. Please."

"Stay here." The man turned his back to them and went deeper into the temple.

Eliezer moved toward a long bench perched up against a nearby wall.

Hadiya followed with hands outstretched. "Now what?"

"Now," he eased his old frame onto the seat, "we wait."

"For how long?"

"Who knows." He shrugged. "The king is a busy man."

Hadiya huffed, threw her back up against the wall, and crossed her arms over her chest.

Rebekah looked apologetically toward Eliezer.

He patted the seat next to himself. "Maybe you should get off your feet."

She shook her head. Though her feet were swollen so much she could no longer distinguish between where her leg ended and where her foot began, sitting was not her child's favorite position. "I'll walk around a bit."

As she made small circles on the worn stone floor, Rebekah noticed the people moving around them. The city dwellers brought in offerings of food, animals, or precious items. Priests accepted gifts and counseled those who had come with questions. An occasional traveler still carrying their packs and coated in dust mixed in with the others.

She looked down at her sand-covered dress. The priest had known right away they weren't from Salem. She guessed he was used to seeing people of all kinds come to the temple. Kicks and punches from inside her caused Rebekah's steps to falter.

Hadiya moved to her side. "Perhaps you should sit down."

Rebekah rubbed the soreness. "Trust me, it doesn't help."

The handmaiden massaged her mistresses' back. "I pray this king can help."

"Me too."

What was probably a very short time, seemed like half a day to Rebekah when the priest who had been sent with word of their arrival finally appeared again. She was glad to see at least the message had reached the king's ear.

The man approached. "Well, I don't know who Abram is, but the king seemed to recognize the name and has moved you to the front of the line. Please follow me. He will see you immediately."

Eliezer nearly flew off the bench and positioned himself beside Rebekah.

She was grateful for the support.

As they moved deeper into the complex, the man led them to a large staircase and began a hasty ascent.

Rebekah hesitated at the bottom. Looking up

toward the top, she swallowed hard.

Hadiya moved to her other side. "We've got you."

With each step, Rebekah's aching feet screamed. She would have preferred to walk into the sun itself than climb a grand staircase on swollen limbs. The pain in her stomach fought for priority over the agony of her burning legs. At some point, the world shifted sideways and she feared passing out.

The hands under each of her arms gripped tighter.

Eliezer whispered in her ear, "Just a few more steps."

She closed her eyes and allowed her two companions to guide her. She simply concentrated on putting one foot in front of the other.

"Last one," Hadiya informed her.

Rebekah set foot on the flat surface and nearly shouted her relief.

"The king won't wait forever." The priest had turned back to call to them.

Rebekah glared at him.

Eliezer adjusted his grip to move closer to her and took on more of her weight. "Don't be upset with the king's servant. Sometimes men speak without thought or observation."

"I was just imagining him pregnant." Rebekah turned to the old servant and moved her eyebrows up and down.

Eliezer chuckled. "I don't think he'd enjoy that at all."

The three travelers followed the man through the doors leading into a main room. At the end of a long path sat an elaborate throne, though Rebekah thought it probably wasn't as proper as the one sitting in the palace.

"Approach," the king's voice boomed from the seat. The construction of the room ensured his voice would carry to every space.

With steeled steps, Rebekah made her way toward the Priest-King.

Melchizedek sat as straight as an arrow upon his seat. Olive skin and worn features revealed him to be a well-traveled man. The paintings of gray hair just above his ears exposed his aging. He was quite handsome, with a little roughness Rebekah was sure he used to keep his city in line.

As they reached him, Eliezer bowed. "Your greatness, I am—"

"Eliezer," the king answered. "I know. I never forget a face." He looked to the two women. "Though I've never seen yours."

Rebekah bowed. "Great King, I am Rebekah. Daughter-in-law to Abra—"

"Daughter-in-law?" The king eyed her and then looked to Eliezer. "Abram finally had a son?"

"Two, in fact, your greatness, and he is called Abraham now."

"Abraham." The new name brought a smile to the king's face. "Two sons certainly don't make one a father of many, now does it?"

"No, your greatness, it doesn't. Though it wasn't Master Abraham's choice to change his name."

"Oh?" He leaned forward. "And whose idea was it?"

"Elohim's."

He eased back. "Was it." He pondered the words for several heartbeats before returning his attention to them. "Well, I've heard you've come to Salem seeking me."

Eliezer pressed Rebekah forward. "It is Rebekah who seeks your wisdom."

"Rebekah?" The king turned his attention toward her with a raised eyebrow.

"Your majesty—" she tried to continue, but the struggle within her increased. She reached for Hadiya and bit down hard on her bottom lip.

Eliezer stepped closer. "Her pain has been increasing."

"Why seek me?" His brow fell. "I don't birth babies."

"No, your greatness, but—"

"I come seeking Elohim!" Rebekah screamed.

Melchizedek's eyebrows shot up. "Why do you come for such a matter as childbearing pain?"

"I need to know what is going on inside me. Even the women who live in our tent city don't understand my pain. They say it's not normal." She clenched her jaw and continued through her teeth, "I know Elohim has all answers. Eliezer believes you would be the one to hear my pleas and take them to Elohim, but more importantly…" she took a deep breath fighting through the torture in her midsection, "…you could hear an answer."

His eyes focused on her.

Rebekah started counting the internal jabs waiting for the king to make a decision.

"I shall inquire on your behalf." He looked to Eliezer. "For Abram—uh— Abraham's sake." He rose.

"Bless you, great king." The old servant bowed deeply.

"Remain here while I prepare an offering. We shall see what Elohim has to say concerning this matter." The king left the room through a side door.

"Help me walk," Rebekah panted.

Hadiya held onto her elbow and guided her around the room.

Rebekah closed her eyes and tried to think of words to say to Elohim. Every prayer she started felt as if she was interrupting the hopeful conversation with Melchizedek. She gave up and started counting the decorative floor tiles as she passed them.

It was more than an hour later when the king returned to his throne.

Rebekah moved toward the seat, expecting him to sit.

He didn't. Instead, he came to stand in front of her. His skin was noticeably lighter and his gaze seemed to be seeing another time or another place.

She couldn't wait any longer. "What did Elohim say?"

A smile played at the corner of his lips as his gaze drifted toward her stomach. His countenance shifted to seriousness. "Congratulations, my dear woman, you are carrying a son."

The words reached her ears and then echoed in her mind. *A son. Isaac's son. He will be so pleased.*

"And another son," the king continued.

"Twins?" she barely whispered the impossible word.

He nodded, keeping his eyes on her stomach.

Twins. She couldn't believe what she was hearing. *Twin boys.*

"But I'm afraid…" his voice trailed off.

The silence ushered in concern as fear wrapped its cold claws around Rebekah's heart. "What?"

His gaze finally moved to meet hers. "I'm afraid the news is not all joyous." His glance shifted far away. "Two nations are in your womb. Two manner of people will be separated from your bowels. The one people will be stronger than the other. The elder shall serve the younger."

"I don't…." Rebekah shook her head. The words didn't make sense. It sounded like some lesson a father would try to teach a son too far beyond his young comprehension. A message wrapped in mystery.

Eliezer moved closer. "Are you sure that's

Elohim's message?"

The king set his firm gaze on the old servant. "I know when Elohim speaks. He was clear. Those were His exact words."

Rebekah wrapped her arms around herself. "But what does it mean?"

"It's true that the pain you've felt is not normal to pregnancy, it is your boys warring with each other. A war that I'm afraid will continue even after they are born."

"Why?" Rebekah watched the king's face twist in pain. His eyes watered, catching the sunlight pouring in from the open windows. Her heart ached as much as her midsection. What terrible words would tumble from his lips next?

"Elohim has separated one of your sons for Himself. He will love one..."

Rebekah's heart lifted. Elohim loved one of her sons. It was too good to hear.

"...but hate the other."

As high as her heart rose, it fell twice as far. "Hate? How could Elohim hate my son before he is even born?"

"Elohim knows us before we take our first breath. He weaves us together in our mother's womb. What right do we have to question His ways?" his voice broke with emotion. "I'm sorry. I know it's not the message you came for, but it's the one you'll have to carry with you. Elohim has spoken."

"Thank you for your time." Eliezer cradled Rebekah's elbow and bowed. "We don't want to keep you."

Rebekah stood still as if her feet had frozen to the tile. She tried to untangle the words from Elohim, but couldn't allow them to sink into her heart. She had prayed for a very long time to bless Isaac with a son of his own. Finally, the fruit of their love had taken hold. Now, this man stood before her telling her Elohim will hate one of her sons. A child who had yet to make a single decision. A child who had yet to take a step in any direction.

"Rebekah," Eliezer's voice brought her back. "We need to find a place to stay for the night. We can travel in the morning."

She shook her head. Words had yet to find their way back to her mouth.

"I can make arrangements for you," the king offered. "She looks like she could use a good night's rest."

"Thank you, Great King." Eliezer bowed.

Hadiya grabbed Rebekah's free arm and helped turn her around.

Rebekah moved her hand to stop them. "Wait." She turned over her shoulder. "Thank you for hearing my pleas."

"I'm glad Elohim answered. He doesn't always." He bowed his head. "I will continue to pray for you, Rebekah."

She nodded and allowed her two servants to escort her from the room.

Chapter 3

*"When her days to give birth were completed,
behold, there were twins in her womb."*
-Genesis 25:24

Beerlahairoi

Two months had passed for Rebekah, though it seemed more like a lifetime. She spent her days pondering the words from Elohim.

"Your hands are still again," Deborah's stern words brought Rebekah's concentration back to the tent.

"Sorry." She adjusted the cloth in her hand to pick up her sewing.

"We need to work quickly if we are going to have enough clothes for two growing boys."

Two boys. There was the thought again. *Elohim will love one and hate the other. Brothers always at war.*

A rough hand covered hers. "Why don't we take a little break? I can cut up some figs for you."

Rebekah attempted a faint smile. "That would be nice."

Deborah put her work to the side and stood to prepare the treat.

Rebekah stared at the wrap in her hand. Soon it would be tucked around one of her boys. The same boys who had spent the last several months causing her pain and fighting with each other.

A tear rolled down her cheek. She'd give anything to have them stay put just so one would never feel separation from Elohim. She remembered what her life was like before she met her husband's family deity. The idols her family worshiped were just stone and wood. They had never brought anything to her life except bartered service and the longing to be accepted.

Elohim had wooed her. He had called to her from her dreams and guided her to the servant who would deliver her into the open arms of her precious husband. He had given her life among people who cared for her. He had blessed her husband and caused their work to prosper. He had planted two seeds in her womb that would give life to her husband.

She cradled her stomach. But one would live without Elohim. More tears traced lines in the sand on her face.

Deborah's arms wrapped around her. "What is it?"

Rebekah wiped her face with the back of her sleeve.

"I'm fine. Just thinking about the boys."

A smile creased the old woman's face. "I can't wait to meet them. They will be truly loved." She patted Rebekah's cheek and went back to her preparations.

Yes, they will. She hugged her midsection. *But not by the One Who matters most.*

Deborah placed a small tray of cut figs at Rebekah's feet.

She picked at the offering, not wanting the gesture to go to waste, but her mind circled like a lost sheep. "What's giving birth like?"

Deborah sat on the floor and picked up her sewing. "I can't speak from experience, but I've watched enough to know it's painful."

"I can't imagine a greater pain than my body has already endured."

She chortled. "That's what all women say."

"How do you know when you're ready?"

"No woman is ever ready. But if you mean when will you know when the time is near, your body will tell you."

She sighed. "I don't think I know what to do when my time comes."

Deborah reached over and patted her hand. "We have many women close by who have walked this path more than once. I'll personally fetch each and every one if it will bring you some measure of peace."

She smiled. "Thank you."

"Now," she patted Rebekah's hand a few more

times, "let's see if we can finish these wraps before the boys arrive."

Rebekah returned her attention to her project, but her mind and body warred as much as the two boys in her womb.

As Rebekah attempted to sleep, the boys inside her continued to protest any and all positions she tried to lay in. She rolled this way and that. She covered and uncovered herself with her wool blanket. Nothing felt good and the boys were more restless than ever.

Not wishing to disturb Isaac, she slipped off the mat and out into the cool night air. She arched her back trying to provide more room to her stomach that seemed to have reached its stretching limit. Her feet ached and her body felt as though she had climbed a mountain only to find another one to scale. Though her body felt tired, her mind was restless.

She waddled around her cooking pit hoping to work through her thoughts enough to sleep. The moon shone brightly on the clear night with a refreshing breeze playing with strands of her hair.

Not knowing exactly why, her steps led her away from her tent and toward the family altar. The simple structure of uncut stone stood against the common night. The flat top was stained with the blood of countless sacrifices to Elohim. Many of those were for the desire of the boys who tussled inside her even at that moment. Prayer turned physical.

They were the answer to her and Isaac's many petitions, but the recent prophecy concerning them only provided more questions.

She stood in the same place she had months before when she fully surrendered to the Stranger who called her. He had become her Shepherd that day and had spoken volumes into her life. Again, she felt humbled by a deity Who would speak to someone like her. The One Who Sees had seen her and given her what she requested. The One Who Hears had answered the question of her condition through the lips of Melchizedek. Would He answer any more?

"Elohim," her lips trembled at even calling His name out loud, "why do You hate my son? A son You formed?" She rubbed the top of her stomach. "Why divide these brothers?"

She reached her hands out to caress the cold stone. "You are a God Who leads and guides, so why separate only one to Yourself?"

Pressing into the stone, she spread her fingers wide trying to pour her request into the place where Elohim might hear.

A still voice echoed in her soul. *Two nations are in your womb. Two manner of people will be separated from your bowels. The one people will be stronger than the other. The elder shall serve the younger.*

She closed her eyes, trying to unwrap the words

and force the understanding to come. The message was simple and clear, but it came with no explanation. She opened her eyes and stared at the dark stains. Should a deity have to explain? Would she understand even if He did?

The pain in her womb shifted to pressure. She bent onto the altar as a wave of tightness pulled her inward.

She rubbed her stomach and tried to straighten. Another wave hunched her back.

"Ow!" her scream echoed in the stillness.

She turned to face the direction of her tent, but another surge halted her steps. Her breath came in short bursts as she attempted to scream. The sound which came forth mimicked a wounded animal.

A few heads popped out of nearby tents followed by bodies heading in her direction.

Hadiya pressed herself through the group heading up the path. "Rebekah, what are you doing out here?" She came to her mistresses' side and held onto her arm. "Are you injured?"

Rebekah could only shake her head back and forth and point to her stomach.

"The babies!" Hadiya's eyes went wide. "Somebody, help me get her back to her tent."

A set of strong arms wrapped around Rebekah's back.

She turned to see Jedidiah, Isaac's most trusted shepherd and faithful friend. His face matched Hadiya's.

"May I?"

She consented with a bob of her head.

He gently scooped her into his arms and rushed her toward the heart of their tent city.

Before Rebekah could blink, she was in her tent surrounded by the people who had shared her life for the last twenty harvest cycles. The air became suffocating with the press of bodies.

"Alright," Deborah's voice called out over the hum of voices, "all of you who've never given birth before please exit this tent. You don't have to go back to your own, but we need to give this woman some space to birth these babies."

"Babies?" the word circled around the crowd.

Rebekah flinched. She had only shared the message of twins and their future with a handful of people. Now, the rest of their fellow laborers and families were aware that more than one child was about to make their arrival.

Deborah waved the men and others out until only a handful of women remained.

Rebekah watched Jedidiah and Isaac leave together. At least her husband would have someone to keep him company while she focused on the difficult task ahead of her.

The old nurse huddled up the few women who chose to remain. "Abigail, since you've had the most children, we'll follow your lead."

Rebekah saw Abigail's gaze flick toward her and

then back to Deborah.

The woman was a few years younger than Rebekah, but she had spent the last twenty providing Jedidiah with more children than his lap could hold. Her father, Yoram, had been the first shepherd Isaac and Jedidiah had hired to help them with the ever-growing flocks. They had been the first to stake their tent next to Isaac and Rebekah. The first in the spreading of the large tent city by the hand of Elohim.

"Of course," the sweet woman agreed. "Gather clean linens and water." Her gentle eyes met Rebekah's. "And anything to make her comfortable. If you're right about more than one baby, it's going to be a long night."

Hours into a difficult labor, Rebekah lay on her side panting.

"I know this is hard," Abigail whispered into her matted hair, "but you're getting so close to holding your first son."

Rays of sunlight poured into the tent practically blinding Rebekah. She squirmed away from the intrusion.

"Shh." Abigail reached a wet rag to Rebekah's sweaty brow. "Just keep breathing."

Though the excruciating pain that ripped at her midsection kept her lips tightly sealed, Rebekah wanted nothing more than to tell Abigail just how irritating her calming voice had become in the fading hours of night. She closed her eyes and tried to focus on slowing her breaths. When another wave tore at her, it was all she could do not to crawl out of her skin and away from the horror that was labor.

"Let's get her up," Abigail's voice snapped her attention.

Deborah and Hadiya moved toward her.

Rebekah shook her head and curled tighter into a ball.

"Rebekah, you need to get up." Abigail put a hand on her arm.

Rebekah swatted her away.

"Trust me, Mistress. It will be much more comfortable to stand."

Her eyes turned into slits as she thought about all the night beasts she could compare the woman to if her voice had not been stolen.

"Child," Deborah's call sliced through the pain. "You do as this woman says right now or so help me, I will swat your bottom right here in this tent."

Rebekah's eyes shot open wide. How dare her own servant speak to her like that. She met the steely glare of the old woman.

Deborah stood with her hands on her broad hips. Her foot tapped out an impatient beat. The woman shifted from servant to second mother in a blink.

At that moment, Rebekah was back to being a little

girl. Despite her agony, her resolve melted. She put her hands under herself and pressed upward.

"Good," Deborah huffed and moved to help her rise.

The three women got Rebekah onto her feet and walking around.

Abigail marched behind her. "When it feels like you have to push, tell us."

Trust me, dear woman, you don't want these lips of mine to part. She gave a sharp nod.

It only took a few circles around the room before Rebekah felt the overwhelming sensation to bear down. She tapped Hadiya's arm.

The handmaiden stopped. "I think she's trying to tell us she's ready."

"Let's move her here to the center." Abigail pointed. "I need you two on either side of her. Johanna, brace her from the back."

Rebekah's two servants and two other women were all who remained from the long night of toil. The rest had retired to get some sleep in order to take care of their own families in the morning.

Rebekah couldn't blame them. She wanted nothing more than to crawl onto her mat and sleep.

Abigail positioned herself under Rebekah. "When you feel like you want to push again, take a deep breath, hold it, then push down."

Rebekah took in a deep breath and kept hold of it. While grasping at Hadiya and Deborah, she bore down as hard as she could.

"Good," Abigail offered. "Let out your breath and wait for the next feeling."

Rebekah blew out all her air and waited.

Hadiya pressed into her ear. "You are doing well. Keep listening to Abigail."

Abigail tapped Rebekah's thigh. "Let's try another one."

Rebekah sucked in a deep breath and held it while she pushed. A scream erupted through her tight lips.

"I can see a head," Abigail's voice rose to a squeal. "Keep going!"

She bore down hard and felt a huge release of pressure.

"Rebekah!" Abigail shouted. "Look at your son."

Sweat dripped down into her eyes, but as she moved her gaze, she saw a blur of red. She blinked her vision clear, but the smear of crimson mixed with other shades of red as if a fire danced among a setting sun. As Abigail slowly guided the baby into a cloth, Rebekah saw a hand wrapped around the red baby's ankle.

Hadiya bent to see what Rebekah was staring at. "Is that the hand of the other baby holding onto his brother?"

"It sure is," Abigail confirmed.

"These boys really do love to fight. No wonder you were in such pain, Mistress."

Abigail reached for a cloth.

Rebekah watched her carefully peel the other

baby's fingers from around his brother's ankle.

Once free of the womb and his brother's grasp, the little red boy let his displeasure of a change of living arrangements be known with a loud cry.

Abigail tied his birth cord with thread to separate the mother from the child. Then she folded the cloth over him, wrapping him up tight. "Johanna, take him while we help the next one."

The woman came from behind Rebekah, took the baby, and cradled him against herself.

"Rebekah," Abigail softened her voice, but kept her gaze firm, "the next one still has his hand out, so it's going to make this a little more uncomfortable."

Rebekah wanted to scoff. She had known heights of discomfort that would send the mightiest warriors crying to their mothers. What were a few more moments?

As the desire of pushing strengthened again, Rebekah felt the burn of the second baby as he tried to enter the breathing world with one arm over his head. She let out scream after scream until the pressure finally eased.

"He's coming."

Rebekah looked down.

Though smeared with blood from delivery and noticeably smaller than his older brother, the second baby was a perfect blend of smooth olive skin and dark hair. His bright almond-shaped eyes shone up at her with brilliance matching the youthfulness of Eliezer's.

Her heart felt like it started beating for the first time. Love poured into her soul and wrapped the two in a bond she could almost see.

Abigail guided the boy's body completely clear and tied his birth cord.

Rebekah couldn't take her eyes off her son. He was even more handsome than his father.

With a quick wrap, Abigail handed the second child to Hadiya. "You've got to keep pushing for me."

Rebekah looked down at her. "I don't understand. Do you think there are more boys?"

She shook her head and cracked a smile. "You've got to deliver their birth sacs."

"More?" Her body ached to lay down as much as her arms ached to hold her perfect bundle.

"It shouldn't take long and nowhere near as painful."

She submitted to her instructions for finishing the birthing process.

When everything was complete and Rebekah was finally permitted to lay down, the women brought the two boys near.

Abigail showed her how to cradle both boys and helped each latch for their first meal.

Rebekah's gaze refused to leave the face of her second son. The more she stared at him, the more beautiful he became.

"You did wonderfully." Abigail smiled.

Rebekah looked up at her. "I do have to apologize."

"For what?"

"I may have thought some awful things toward you through the night."

"Don't worry." She waved her off. "All words and thoughts are forgiven during labor. I got through mine by imagining a falcon plucking out my mother-in-law's eyes if she told me to breathe one more time."

Rebekah let out a long, hard belly laugh as she watched her two boys suckle away.

"Have you and Isaac talked about names?"

She shook her head. "I didn't want to even imagine until they were here."

The bulky, crimson bundle that lay in her arms wiggled against her. Her firstborn son looked more like a wild beast than a baby. He reminded her of a desert lynx. Sandy-red hair coated his body from head to toe and his eyes were round and wild. Even his ears were slightly pointed, adding to the image of the bulky desert cat.

"Esau," the only name that seemed to match the appearance of the boy in her arms came over her lips.

"Well," Hadiya attempted to smooth the baby's wild, red locks, "he is a bit hairy."

"And the other?" Abigail wondered.

Rebekah was trapped again in the penetrating gaze of her younger son. "Jacob."

The women around her laughed.

Hadiya shook her head. "I don't think any of us are going to forget that little fist held tight to his brother's ankle."

Rebekah tried to adjust both boys.

Esau dropped his latch and let everyone know his displeasure with a loud cry.

"This is going to take some practice," she tried not to let frustration damper the moment.

"It will." Deborah carefully scooped Esau into her arms and began to nurse the child herself. "You brought me along for a reason and I've been waiting all this time to do what I was kept around for." She winked.

Rebekah stared at the old woman with fresh amazement. "I didn't think it possible."

"Just like Master Isaac says, 'Elohim doesn't believe in the word impossible.' "

Chapter 4

"The first came out red, all his body like a hairy cloak,
so they called his name Esau. Afterward his brother
came out with his hand holding Esau's heel, so his
name was called Jacob. Isaac was sixty years old when
she bore them."
-Genesis 25:25-26

Beerlahairoi, 1995 B.C.

Rebekah sat beside her cooking fire watching her two
young boys run together in the open field.

Her aging dog, Ashen, kept a close eye on the boys
as he could no longer keep up with his own children
and grandchildren that protected the herds. He made
sure the boys did not wander too far from the tent city.

Ten years had blessed each son with growth and
strength, but it seemed to Rebekah that they grew in
two different directions. Though born within
moments of each other, the two boys were as different

as the sun and moon, day and night, a mountain and a river, a goat and a sheep.

Her oldest son, Esau, was covered from head to toe in sandy-red hair as rough as goat's hair. And he was just as ornery as one. Sometimes Rebekah swore she could see goat horns sprouting through his crimson mane. His fiery hair matched his fiery personality. Just like the sun or a breaking day, no one could deny his presence. He didn't let anything stand in his way and if something tried, he stood against it until it moved like a looming mountain that bent for no man.

Jacob was just the opposite. He was smooth-skinned and, what hair he had, was as black as night and smooth as sheep's wool. As calm as a cool river and as still as night, Jacob never let anything bother him. As much as his brother tried, Jacob was never rustled by his brother's pestering. He was Rebekah's moon. Steady. The bright spot in her life that drove away any darkness that tried to claim her attention.

Esau wrapped his arm around Jacob's neck and tossed him to the ground. The older and bigger boy coiled around his younger brother like a viper, tossing him around in the sand.

Rebekah could only sigh as she watched the familiar sight. It wasn't their first battle and certainly would not be their last. She had broken up the first hundred, but Isaac demanded she stop. He wanted his boys to become strong men and, in his eyes, that would never happen if their mother settled their disagreements for them. Though the fights were never settled, they always ended when Jacob yielded to the power of his older brother.

Abigail passed by with a basket of freshly cleaned clothes on her head. "Are those two at it again?"

"Always."

She plopped her wash down and put her hands on her hips. "If you ask me, those boys could use a few more good swats to their bottoms."

"Tried it." She sighed again. "Nothing seems to keep those two from their personal war."

"Sorry." Abigail's stature softened. "I know from personal experience that kids who don't seem to get along can make it rough on their mother."

Rebekah smiled. She remembered Abigail breaking up more than one of her ten children's fights over the years.

"Well, let's hope they grow out of the desire to harm one another as quickly as mine seem to." She shook her head. "Though I still catch the two youngest of my boys testing each other's physical limits."

She nodded. *Hope.* She had hoped to get pregnant. She had hoped to live in peace and blessing. She had hoped for a lot of things. Could she still hold on to the hope of one day seeing her two warring sons stand side by side as friends instead of enemies?

"You know," Rebekah began, staring at the two boys, "it's almost as if they sprang from different seeds."

Abigail looked to the boys and back to her. "What do you mean?"

"I was just sitting here thinking about how very different they are, but they grew in me at the same time." She chewed on her inside cheek. "My gentle Jacob would much rather spend his time among the flocks with his father or cooking next to me, while Esau follows after the men who hunt. It's almost as if the thrill of killing drives him and nothing else. They are different in appearance... in speech... in almost every way two people can be different. And yet...yet they are birth brothers."

"It certainly is a mystery." Abigail picked up her basket and strolled toward her tent.

Two nations are in your womb. The prophetic words of Elohim resounded in her mind again. *Two manner of people will be separated from your bowels. The one people will be stronger than the other. The elder shall serve the younger.*

Rebekah watched Jacob yield to his brother once again. *The elder shall serve the younger.*

The shuffle of feet approaching caused her to turn around. Two familiar old men stood with smiles spread wide.

She rose to embrace them. "Abraham! Eliezer! It is good to see you."

"Always good to be seen." Abraham chuckled.

"And to see you, Mistress Rebekah," Eliezer added.

"To what do we owe this wonderful surprise?" She

watched the servant's gaze flick to his master.

Abraham waved his hand. "Just wanted to see those growing grandchildren of mine." He passed her.

Rebekah raised an eyebrow at Eliezer.

He mouthed, "Later."

She nodded to let him know she understood.

"Great *Abba* Abraham!" the two boys shouted and ran in their direction, toppling their grandfather to the ground with affection.

His laughter erupted as Rebekah worried if his older frame could bear the weight of the growing boys. He rolled in the sands with them, tussling their hair, and doing his best to pin each one to the ground. "You boys are as slippery as eels and better fighters than your *abba*." He stood and dusted sand from his gray hair.

"Yeah, but I'm much better," Esau prided himself and added a leap onto Jacob in an effort to start another round of scuffling.

"Why don't you boys go practice some more while you give this old man a rest?"

Esau's countenance fell. "Aww, but I want to play with you."

"Do as your Great *Abba* says," Rebekah corrected. "He'll come play with you soon."

"Yes, *Ima*." The older boy sulked away.

"I'm so glad you've come for a visit," Jacob beamed. "We've missed you."

Abraham smiled and rubbed his hand into the boy's dark hair. "Me too, child, me too." He patted the young boy's shoulder. "Now, why don't you go play. I'll be along shortly."

Jacob rushed off to follow his brother.

Rebekah shook her head.

Abraham moved to sit by the roaring fire.

"Hadiya," Rebekah called.

The handmaiden stepped from the tent. "Yes?"

"Would you prepare something for our guests, please?"

She looked at the two men with a bright smile. "Of course. It would be an honor."

"I've always liked her." Eliezer winked at Rebekah.

"Me too." She chuckled. "So, what brings you two to the south?"

"Just as I said," Abraham's voice took on a stern edge, "I wanted to see these boys before they grow right out of my life."

Rebekah watched his hard exterior bend slightly. "Boys often do."

"Speaking of boys," he shook off his far-off stare, "where is my son Isaac?"

"I expect the shepherds to be home any day now. They seem to stay out later every year." She shrugged. "Or it could just be that I miss him more and more."

The sight of the family's altar caught Abraham's attention. He motioned toward it with his chin. "He still offering sacrifices to Elohim?"

"Every day he's home." She beamed. "And he taught the boys to do so while he's away."

45

"Soon they'll be out there with him."

Rebekah's heart constricted. She knew first-hand what dangers lay in the wilderness. "That's a heated topic for us."

Abraham turned to face her. "Oh?"

"Esau has already asked not to follow."

"What does the boy expect to do if not to take on his father's trade?"

Rebekah swallowed hard. "I'm afraid he desires only to hunt. Much to my disapproval, he sneaks off with the hunters as much as he can. Several of them have encouraged the behavior."

Abraham rubbed at his long beard. "And Jacob?"

"Jacob loves the flocks." She smiled. "I see so much of Isaac and me in him." Her smile faded. "I'm afraid it has been by my insistence that he hasn't yet gone on a wilderness trip with his father. Though he does help during the cold months and even learned to birth lambs."

Thoughts of her mother flooded over her. The tight hold Kishar had on Rebekah's younger brother, Laban, now made sense. Mother to mother, she knew why her grasp had been so tight. She now understood the desire to never let go.

Abraham looked at her as if he could read her thoughts. "You must let them go at some point."

"I know." She fought the rising lump in her throat. "I know. I was younger than they are when I went on my first trip with my *abba*..." Images of her loving father taken all too soon from her life flashed in her mind and stole her voice. She missed him. She knew he would have loved to meet his grandchildren. Tears blurred her vision.

The two men sat silently waiting for her to compose herself.

"Sorry." She wiped her face.

Hadiya appeared with trays of fresh fruit, warm bread, and tea. "Enjoy." She departed with a proper bow.

Abraham offered a simple blessing and tasted of the treats.

A thought entered Rebekah's mind that captured her attention. "*Abba* Abraham?"

"Yes, child?"

"Did you really see Elohim?"

Eliezer choked on the piece of bread he had popped into his mouth. He emptied a cup of tea in an attempt to clear the blockage.

After making sure his servant was well, Abraham turned his attention back to her. "I did."

"And Elohim spoke to you?"

His stare seemed to travel over the years and distance. "Spoke. Promised. Warned." He fixed his stare on her.

She let her gaze drift away as she thought on his words.

"Has Elohim spoken to you?"

She ducked her head. "I believe He used to call to

me from my dreams until I met Isaac. Since then I only… feel Him."

Abraham nodded in complete understanding.

"But when I was pregnant, I went to see King Melchizedek."

"Eliezer told me."

"Did he tell you what he said?"

Abraham shook his head. "Just that you had gone to inquire of Elohim." He turned a glare on his servant. "Even as many times as I attempted to retrieve the information from my most trusted servant."

Eliezer beamed. "Some messages are meant only for their recipient."

"Well," Rebekah began, "Elohim answered my inquiry. But I don't understand it."

A broad smile spread across the wrinkles of Abraham's weathered face. "That is something I know all too well."

"Melchizedek told me that Elohim said, 'Two nations are in your womb. Two manner of people will be separated from your bowels. The one people will be stronger than the other. The elder shall serve the younger.' "

Abraham pondered the words. "They certainly are two very different boys. Though I don't ever see Esau bowing to Jacob. It would be like a mountain bending to a river."

"That's not the part that concerns me."

He lifted a brow.

"Elohim also said He would love one and hate the other."

"Hate?"

She bowed her head. The word still stung at her insides.

"I can see your apprehension." He played with the ends of his frayed beard.

She turned to watch Esau and Jacob wrestle. They grew bigger every day, but they were still so young. "How can Elohim hate a little boy?"

Abraham shrugged. "I know a lot about Elohim, but I don't know everything. You see, things are different with Him. We commune. We have a... relationship." He held up his gnarled, aged hands. "None of the gods I made with these ever desired a relationship with me." He slowly lowered them. "They required unquestioned service. Elohim first requests our love, then our service."

She tried to make his words fit with the prophecy that hung over the heads of her sons.

"Maybe," Abraham held up a curled finger, "maybe He knows Esau will never love Him."

"But how can that be? Isaac and I show Esau every day of his life the goodness of Elohim and how to serve Him."

"I did the same for Lot, yet he never chose Elohim for himself."

The idea of her young son following in Lot's twisted steps made her stomach turn. "What if he never does?"

"Some do." Abraham leaned back. "Some don't."

It was nearly three days later when the shepherds returned to the tent city.

The women, children, and elder members welcomed them back with a grand feast with Abraham as an honored guest.

Late into the evening, Abraham leaned over the table near Rebekah, "Have you returned home to visit your family since marrying my son?"

She shook her head. "I send word on occasion. A messenger is expensive for such a distance. My brother has only sent one to inform me of the death of our mother."

"How sad. Family shouldn't have to live so far apart."

As he leaned back, she caught the glance of Eliezer. Something in his look told her there was a deeper meaning to Abraham's words. She remembered the servant had something private to share with her and she had yet to make the time to hear him. "I'm going to go check on the next round of platters. Eliezer, would you help me?"

He rose quickly and followed silently after her.

When they were removed from the noisy feast, she stopped and spun around. "Tell me."

He waited.

"What is going on with Abraham?"

Eliezer stood still.

"I know you wanted to tell me something." She appraised the way he shifted under her words.

"There is something Abraham wants to ask Isaac. He is waiting for the right time."

"Ask him what?"

He sighed. "Abraham fears his days are short. He wants your family to move to Hebron until he dies so he can be close to his family."

Rebekah put her hand over her heart. "I had no idea."

"He's not frightened of death." The servant straightened his shoulders. "He only wants to fill his last days with the things that bring him the most joy. His sons from Keturah have grown and taken wives, some moved away. He misses Isaac. He wants to be part of Esau's and Jacob's lives."

"I can understand that."

"Can you?" His eyes misted.

She softened. "Of course."

"This is possibly the last request of his I can help fulfill."

"I will do all in my power to make sure Isaac understands the urgency."

The two made their way back to the feast.

Rebekah returned to her husband's side as he was engaged in a lively discussion of sheep with his father.

She smiled and laughed along with them.

Then Abraham got quiet.

She noticed him mull over the thing that weighed on his heart and mind.

"Son..." he started, but waited for Isaac's full attention.

Isaac put down his cup and turned toward Abraham. "*Abba*?"

"You know none of us get to outlive the sun." He put his hands on the table and rested on them to lean closer to his son. "I have a request that I hope you won't deny an old, maybe foolish, man."

"I would do anything for you, *Abba*. All I have is because of you." He looked to Rebekah.

"Well, me and Elohim." He waved his hand around. "But that's beside the point." He eased back. "I want you and your family to come live with me in Hebron."

Isaac's mouth hung open. He shook his head, then closed his mouth. "Why? My whole life is here... my flocks are here... my—"

Abraham put up a hand. "Not forever. Just until Elohim decides to take my last breath."

Rebekah watched concern reach Isaac's face.

"*Abba*, are you ill?"

The old man waved his hands in front of himself. "Nothing like that. I just know I don't have many days left." He looked to Rebekah. "I want to spend them with the ones I care about." He turned back to his son.

"I want to fill my ears with the sounds of those two boys of yours playing and laughing."

Isaac looked around. "I just don't know how I can walk away from all this."

"Jedidiah," Rebekah offered.

The men turned toward her.

"You trust him with your life, surely you can trust him with your flocks until we return."

"You want to leave?" His face scrunched and twisted as if she were betraying him.

"I don't want to leave our home." She put a gentle hand on his arm. "But speaking as one who left home behind for a bigger adventure before," she smiled, "I would love to bless your *abba* with time." She turned her bright grin on Abraham. "Time to spend with his grandchildren and time spent with us."

Isaac shook his head. "I don't know."

"It is something I wish every day I could bless my *abba* with," her voice broke with emotion. She swallowed hard.

Isaac covered her hand with his and patted it gently. "I concede. We'll go."

Rebekah glanced at Abraham.

His smile beamed wide enough to be seen from the next table.

She shifted her attention to Eliezer.

His head was bowed, but she caught the reflection of a single tear streaming down his cheek.

Chapter 5

*"These are the days of the years of Abraham's life,
175 years... After the death of Abraham, God blessed
Isaac his son. And Isaac settled at Beer-lahai-roi."*
-Genesis 25:7, 11

Hebron, 1990 B.C.
Jacob

Jacob twisted the freshly cleaned wool between his fingers. A movement he had done so many times he could probably finish the entire basket next to him with his eyes closed.

Zeve, his trusted herd dog, lay on the other side fast asleep as the familiar hum of family life buzzed in the large tent.

The three women Jacob loved most, his mother, her handmaid, and his nurse, all worked together like a pack of wolves devouring each task in front of them. Sometimes he didn't know where one woman ended and the other began.

He reached into the pile of wool to continue the strand in his hand. While he worked, his mind wandered. The cold days had sent the sheep and shepherds from the wilderness to the tent city. He was restless to return to his duty in the fields, but there was much work to be done at home while they waited.

Five harvest seasons ago, his family had moved from Beerlahairoi to pitch their tent with his grandfather, Abraham. With the move, his mother had finally given permission for Jacob to join his father and the other shepherds to work with Abraham's flocks. It was the height of his happiness. Ever since he could remember, he wanted to be a shepherd like his father.

He looked up at his mother.

Rebekah glanced at him over her shoulder and smiled.

Jacob knew she enjoyed having him home. The woman could barely contain the ridiculous grin that became permanently fixed on her face when they arrived home every time the weather cooled.

She put on a strong appearance the first time he followed his father toward the wilderness. However, Jacob knew her well enough to know she probably spent the first several nights he was away crying— and praying. His mother was always praying. Several of his family members prayed. But his mother's prayers always felt as if he were scooped up into the presence of Elohim Himself. It was something he longed for, even attempted to imitate, but could never make true in his innermost parts.

Another bundle ran through his fingers lengthening the thread.

The tent flap flung open wide as Esau clamored inside and flopped a fairly large fallow deer from his shoulder to the ground. He straightened, nearly grazing the top of the tent with his head.

If there was one thing, and one thing only, that Jacob envied about the brother he had shared a womb with it was his size. Though born only moments behind him, Jacob was almost half the height and weight of his older brother. Of course, almost every man was smaller than Esau. Even their father and grandfather had been recently dwarfed by the rapidly rising boy.

Esau wiped his face clear of sweat only to leave smears of blood in its place.

"Esau!" Rebekah scolded. "What have I told you about bringing kills into this home?"

He looked down at the animal, then back to her with a shrug.

"I've asked you time and time again to clean your kills before you drag them in here. That blood is going to attract every predator within miles."

He moved toward her and wrapped her in a grip as tight as a viper. Her feet lifted off the woven carpets as he spun her around. "But isn't she a beauty, *Ima*?"

"Yes, yes, yes." She swatted at his muscled arm.

"Now put me down."

He dropped her a little too hard, causing her feet to stumble. As he attempted to right her, he knocked into Deborah who dropped a bowl of dried figs.

One of the round treats rolled next to Jacob's foot and he quickly popped it into his mouth.

"Esau!" Deborah huffed.

The boy's face turned crimson. "I'm sorry." He tried to reach down to pick up the bowl and knocked heads with his mother who was attempting the same.

"Ow!" Rebekah squealed as her hand flew to her forehead.

"I'm sorry, *Ima*!"

She reached out for him. "I'm well." She patted his arm and then grasped the bowl and handed it to Deborah. "Why don't you get to work cleaning your kill… outside."

He tucked his head. "Yes, *Ima*." With a gentle kiss to the top of her head, he picked up the deer and retreated.

Hadiya moved to examine Rebekah. Her thin fingers pressed into the already rising lump. "I'll mix you up something for that."

"Thank you." Rebekah lightly fingered the bump.

Deborah bent down to gather the dropped fruit. "That boy better learn to control that body of his."

"You can't blame him." Rebekah sighed. "His body scarcely has time to adjust before it shoots up again."

"He may be as big as a mountain," Jacob added,

"but he seems to have one growing in his head as well."

"Jacob!" Rebekah spun around to him and put her hands on her hips. "Don't speak about your brother in such a manner."

He ducked his head, but couldn't cease laughing. "Sorry, *Ima*." When he lifted his gaze, he saw a spark of amusement dance in her eyes despite her wagging head.

A commotion outside brought all of their attention up and toward the tent flap.

The familiar voice of Abraham's wife, Keturah rang out, "Rebekah!"

Jacob dropped his thread and hopped to his feet. He watched his mother position herself to flee the tent, but the older woman entered in a whirl.

"Rebekah! Rebekah!" Keturah rushed toward her, nearly knocking her over. She grasped madly at her arms. "Where is Isaac? I can't find him."

"He went into Hebron this morning." She tried to loosen the grasp of the hysterical woman. "He'll be back soon."

"It's Abraham."

With those simple words, Jacob felt his heart dip into his stomach. "What's wrong with Great *Abba* Abraham?"

Keturah turned her wild gaze on him. "He's dead."

The air left Jacob's chest and he fought to bring in more. He shook his head and marched through the tent flap.

His feet swiftly took him the familiar few steps toward his grandfather's simple tent. It was a trail he had traveled more times than he could probably count. Whether he needed advice, prayer, or some place to retreat from his infuriating brother, Jacob's path undoubtedly led to his grandfather.

Eliezer, his grandfather's servant, sat outside the tent knelt in the sand. He was tossing handfuls of dirt onto his head and wailing. Streaks of tears ran tracks in the dust on his old cheeks.

Jacob pressed past him and into the tent.

There, still lying on his reed mat under a goat-skin blanket, lay Abraham. He was tranquil, almost as if merely asleep.

Jacob's steps lightened as he edged closer. Slowly, he knelt and reached for Abraham's exposed hand. It wasn't cold, but it wasn't warm with life either. He shook it, but it just rolled from side to side.

"Great *Abba*?" he whispered.

Nothing.

He shook his grandfather's arm harder. "Please." His eyes burned, but he refused to give in to their pleas to dampen.

With trembling fingers, he reached over to place his palm just over his grandfather's face.

No breath warmed his hand.

The room felt more deserted than it should. The intangible thing that made Abraham his grandfather was noticeably gone. It was as if he were looking upon an empty chaff instead of the vibrant man he respected and admired.

He shut his eyes and willed the morning to be a nightmare from which he could arise.

The sound of footsteps rushing behind him caused his eyes to open.

His mother stood just inside the tent.

She moved slowly as if trying not to spook a frightened animal. "I sent Hadiya to fetch your *abba* and Deborah went to find Esau."

He could hear Keturah's cries intertwine with Eliezer's on the other side of the tent wall.

Rebekah reached over and wiped at his cheek with her knuckle.

He hadn't felt the dampness fall until her touch.

"Your great *abba* has seen many a harvest." She spread her palm on his cheek. "Many more than most."

He closed his eyes and pressed into her hand. The tears came freely. He felt her other arm wrap around him and pull him close.

She rocked him in a rhythmic sway she hadn't done since he had outgrown her lap.

The reassurance of his mother's embrace was interrupted by the entrance of several family members.

First Esau, who took one look at his grandfather's body and left.

Isaac entered next. His cheeks were flushed as if he had run the short distance without a single breath from the stone city that shadowed their tents.

Deborah and Hadiya came in, but stood near the far tent wall as a sign of respect.

Jacob sat wrapped in his mother's arms still wishing for the bad dream to cease.

It wasn't until they began the burial wrappings that Jacob finally unwound himself and crawled to the edge of the room. By then, the air around them had been suffocated with the sounds of wailing as word of the patriarch's death had spread through the camp.

Isaac came to sit next to him.

The two men sat in silence as they watched the preparations.

It was Jacob who broke the stillness, "Where will you bury him?"

"Machpelah, with my *Ima* Sarah."

Jacob never met his grandfather's first wife, but the old man loved to share stories of her.

"I need to ask a favor of you, my son."

He kept his eyes on the hands of the women.

"I need to send you to Kadesh."

He turned then. "What's in Kadesh?"

"Your *dod*."

Jacob shook his head. "But *Dods* Zimran, Jokshan, Medan, Midian, Ishbak, and Shuah don't live in Kadesh."

"Not them." Isaac met his questioning glare. "Your *Dod* Ishmael is my *abba's* firstborn. It is required that he be here for the burial." He rolled his shoulders inward. "I have never been very good at keeping up with him beyond replacing his guard dog when needed. I guess I always felt… inferior…" He looked up at his son. "Whatever the past holds, it's right that he be here. I need someone I can trust with the message for him to come."

"Of course, *Abba*," Jacob heard the words come from his mouth before he thought them.

"I'll send Jedidiah with you. He'll know where to find him." His eyes misted. "You shouldn't be alone." Slowly his gaze drifted back to the center of the room. "None of us should be alone right now."

Jacob rose and left the tent. If it was his duty to fetch a faraway uncle, he was going to waste no time in retrieving him. He tipped-toed around prostrate bodies surrounding the tent. Men and women threw dirt on themselves causing the air to fill with dust. It was almost too much to breathe.

He escaped the hoard only to notice one body was noticeably absent from the gathering. His search led him to the edge of the tent city.

About a stone's throw away, Esau knelt in the field cleaning his morning kill.

Jacob approached. "Why aren't you mourning?"

His older brother kept his focus on his blood-covered hands. "What is there to mourn?" He shrugged. "Old men die."

Jacob felt heat rise from the center of his body and race up his neck and into his face. "And foolish boys continue to live their foolish lives."

Esau threw down his knife and rose to his full height, towering over Jacob. "Watch your tongue, or I shall relieve you of it."

Jacob felt saliva pool in his mouth. He wanted nothing more than to spit in his brother's face, but he knew the act would definitely lead to a physical battle he was certain to lose. Again. Especially against a hunter seething from a victorious hunt.

He bit down hard on his lip, tasting blood. He continued to chew, fighting against the rise of words that tried to claw their way out. With more important tasks to accomplish than wasting time with a boulder-headed brother, he turned and went to his mother's tent to pack.

Jacob gathered the few supplies he needed and slung the bag over his shoulder.

The tent flap moved to reveal Rebekah.

"Your father tells me he's sending you to Ishmael." He nodded.

"Take this." She handed him a squirming bundle.

"Nissa?" Jacob inspected the young Kangal pup. She was the prized female from their last litter his mother had looked forward to raising. "I don't understand."

"I'm sure Ishmael's previous dog is past her service days." She shrugged. "I'm surprised we haven't had a visit from him before now." Her fingers moved to rub between the dog's ears. "Nissa here will make a fine watchdog. And I'm hoping she will buy your favor for

Ishmael to accept your *abba's* request to come."

"Why would I need favor with Great *Abba's* son?"

She didn't take her eyes off the wiggling dog. "There is a lot we haven't shared with you." Her gaze lifted. "I suppose there is much to speak of when the burial is complete."

Jacob hugged the puppy closer to his body. What buried secrets would be unearthed when he returned with an uncle he just discovered lived only a few cities away?

Chapter 6

"As for Ishmael, I have heard you; behold, I have blessed him and will make him fruitful and multiply him greatly. He shall father twelve princes, and I will make him into a great nation."
-Genesis 17:20

Kedesh

Jacob was grateful that Jedidiah wasn't much of a talker. They had shared the last few journeys together through the wilderness. It made for a comfortable silence in which Jacob could rehearse his father's request.

When the city of Kedesh came into view, Jacob paused.

"Don't worry," Jedidiah slapped Jacob's back, "we come as messengers, not as enemies."

Jacob swallowed the rising bile and willed his heart to slow its rapid pace. He had never been trusted with an important message before. What if his uncle refused because of him?

Jedidiah's steady steps took them through the streets of Kedesh toward an impressive villa.

Jacob had seen some large houses in Hebron, but the structure before him could rival the temples in the city next to his family's tents.

A deep bark from somewhere in the courtyard alerted the guards to their approach.

Jacob watched an elderly dog march toward them as if she carried the same sword and armor as her fellow laborers who flanked her rear. The hair around her muzzle was as white as snow, but the rest of her golden fur and massive build reminded him of the dogs he helped his family raise. This is what his mother must have meant. His father provided watchdogs to his uncle.

He tightened his grip on the puppy in his hand who attempted to engage in play with the fellow dog. She pawed and yipped. Little did the puppy know the other dog wasn't interested in play, but trained to attack anything not invited in by the master of the house. The poor pup would find herself in the jaws of a skilled killer if Jacob let her down.

"State your business," the older-looking guard barked. The touches of gray above his ears matched the color of the dog's muzzle.

"W-w-we come bearing gifts and a message for Ishmael from Isaac." Jacob cursed the tremble in his voice and hoped his tunic hid the one rising in his legs.

The guard's bushy brow lifted as his eyes examined the two men before him. "Wait here." He turned and marched back into the courtyard.

Standing as still as a statue, the other guard's glare bored holes into them. The dog stood with her head slightly bent down and shoulders poised to pounce. A low growl rumbled through her clenched teeth.

Jacob couldn't blame either sentinel for their stance. He and his companion were uninvited trespassers. They had every right to be wary. Though the more he reasoned out what his eyes took in, nothing seemed to calm the quake in his knees or the bile that threatened to spill his simple meal of bread and figs from his stomach and onto the guard's sandals. He shifted his focus to keeping the wiggling puppy in his arms. His mother would never forgive him if her best dog was killed by an unknown relative.

The older guard returned. "Let them in."

With a swift movement, the second gave a hand signal for the dog to withdraw.

Only when she had backed away and was properly seated next to the first, did the man unlatch the gate.

He waved them in and secured the gate behind them. "Step quickly and don't make eye contact with the dog."

Jacob moved the fidgeting pup to his chest and held her tight. He kept his eyes straight ahead. As they passed the first guard, he could hear the warning growl still rumble from the older dog.

The man led them through the courtyard and toward a large open area.

Standing there was an older version of Jacob's father. He was a mix of Isaac and Abraham, though his skin was much darker.

"When my guard informed me of a messenger at my gate from my brother, I did not imagine a boy," Ishmael's deep voice carried through the space.

It almost stopped Jacob's advance, but Jedidiah continued near.

"And an old shepherd." Ishmael laughed. "Welcome, Jedidiah."

Jedidiah halted and bowed low. "We are honored to be heard. May I present Isaac's son, Jacob." He waved beside him.

Jacob bowed, but not before he watched Ishmael's face expand outward as if his chin and brows were trying to flee each other.

"Isaac's son?" Ishmael repeated. "Only son?"

Jacob straightened. "I have a twin brother."

"Two sons." He clapped and rubbed his palms together. "How I wish I would have received word." His appearance hardened.

"Forgive your brother," Jedidiah hurried to explain. "His flocks grow larger than he can manage some seasons. Things often get…"

Jacob watched his fellow shepherd falter. The man shouldn't speak ill of his master, but what other explanation could he offer to cool the obvious slight.

Ishmael held up his hand. "Peace." He shook his head. "I know my brother well enough to understand." His deep gaze turned toward Jacob. "And what of you, young man. You must have seen what? Fourteen harvests by now."

"Fifteen," he corrected.

"My mistake." Ishmael chuckled. "Fifteen. Almost a man." He looked to the squirming bundle in Jacob's arms. "And what do we have there?"

Jacob held the puppy out. "She is a gift. My *ima* Rebekah sends her along with her blessing."

"Ahh." He received the dog into his arms. "Rebekah is a true beauty inside and out. One that rivals any found in Egypt." He winked toward Jedidiah.

The puppy licked at his mouth.

"She is fair too. But I don't understand," he shook his head, "why does this gift come without call? I would have visited my brother when my female had passed on just as I had last time."

Jacob looked to Jedidiah.

The older shepherd closed his eyes and bowed his head.

As much as he didn't want to, the message was Jacob's to deliver. The faithful laborer would not willingly take the responsibility upon himself. No matter how much Jacob silently pleaded.

Jacob swallowed hard and turned to face Ishmael. He silently commanded his voice to stay firm. "We have a message from Isaac."

Ishmael's brows knitted together. "The dog is not the message?"

Jacob shook his head. "She is an offering of peace and blessing. My *ima* hoped she might open your ears to our words."

"Speak on."

Jacob took a breath and locked his wavering knees. "Abraham is dead."

Ishmael took a step back, nearly dropping the puppy from his arms. He recovered enough to grip her before she tumbled to the tiled floor. "Dead?"

Jacob's gaze shifted to the floor.

"I knew him to be an old man." He shook his head as if trying to get water out of his ears. "I knew the day had to come, but…" his deep voice trailed off.

Jacob glanced at Jedidiah who stood perfectly still with his eyes closed. He looked back to his uncle whose stare was far away.

Only the dog in his uncle's arms moved for what felt like days.

Ishmael finally returned his focus to the room. "Jacob, I'm sorry you had to deliver this news." He bowed his head. "You are so young to lose such an important part of your life. Despite the past, I knew Abraham as a great man. I'm sure he was a wonderful Great *Abba* to you."

The tremor that lived in Jacob's knees now jumped to his throat. Emotions tore at him. He couldn't show them to this warrior-man who shared his lifeblood. "He was. I've spent the past five harvests traveling with him and his shepherds through the wilderness. He taught me much."

"Count it a blessing."

"There is more."

Ishmael held tight to the dog. "Speak."

"My *abba* has demanded you return with us to oversee the burial."

With a deep shake of his head, he hardened. "I don't think I'd be very welcomed."

"You are not only welcomed, but requested. *Abba* told me not to return without you. He said…" Jacob rehearsed his father's words, " 'Whatever the past holds, it's right that he be here.' "

Ishmael spent several heartbeats considering the words.

"And I would like very much for the chance to get to know one of my *dods*," Jacob added.

He brightened.

"And you can meet your other brothers."

He tilted his head. "Brothers?"

"Six to be exact. Word has been sent for them to gather as well."

Ishmael chuckled. "So, Abraham became the father of many after all."

"Does that mean you accept the offer?"

He smiled. "I will come."

Jacob felt his heart slow to a steady pace for the first

time since he left his mother's tent.

"But first we need to have this girl meet her companion and I'm sure you two would enjoy a meal with me. We shall travel with first light to Beerlahairoi."

"To Hebron."

"Hebron?"

"Great *Abba* Abraham is to be buried in Machpelah, but *Abba* pitched his tent by Hebron five harvests ago by request of Abraham."

"I see. Then to Hebron it is."

Jacob followed his uncle deeper into his home with pride filling each step. He would bring the distant son to bury his father. Jacob had accomplished his task. His father would be pleased.

Chapter 7

"Isaac and Ishmael his sons buried [Abraham] in the cave of Machpelah, in the field of Ephron the son of Zohar the Hittite, east of Mamre,"
-Genesis 25:9

Machpelah

The caravan of people beat the rising sun to the cave.

Jacob stood beside his mother watching Isaac and Ishmael reunite. His father held tight to his uncle as they both wept in full view of the entire gathering. Their cries were drowned in the sea of sorrow that surrounded them.

People from nearby cities joined their family's procession from Hebron to Machpelah as word spread through the land of Abraham's death. A mix of colors, beliefs, and statuses blended in the song of mourning for the man who had a lasting impact on all he met.

Jacob stood with locked legs focusing on the stone

blocking the entrance to the cave. His lips were held still by the numbness that stole his wails. His eyes burned, but didn't dampen. His heart ached, but felt as if it were simply an empty almond shell buried in dry ground.

Large men moved toward the boulder at Isaac's command. The massive stone gave way easily to the grip of the men.

Women all around covered their faces with veils to relieve their delicate noses of the scent that permeated from inside.

Jacob held his breath hoping to keep the stench at bay; the aroma of death.

Isaac and Ishmael walked toward the cart that held the prepared body of their father. The women had taken extra care to wrap Abraham with linens rubbed with oils and spices. The fragrance masked the odor of rot, but didn't hide it completely.

The brothers lifted the body and walked together toward the cave.

Rebekah took a shaky step toward them.

Jacob slipped his hand under her elbow without looking at her.

She eased into his frame as they walked.

He felt her sobs reverberate through her whole body. Without turning around, he heard the clomping of Esau's giant feet slapping against his sandals behind them. Keturah followed close as if drifting on the breeze. Her headwrap was wet from drying her endless tears.

The small group entered the cave and moved through the first chamber and into the second.

While Jacob had gone to Kedesh to fetch his uncle, men from his family had hewn a place for Abraham's body next to the only other burial shelf in the chamber.

Laying neatly wrapped with linens discolored from age was the remains of Abraham's first wife, Sarah.

Jacob paused as they passed her. Stories of her beauty and love flooded his mind. His Great *Abba* enjoyed sharing them freely and repeatedly. The love of his life and the mother of his beloved son, Sarah was a woman whose fame lingered even though her decaying body lay still on the cool stone.

As Isaac and Ishmael lifted the body of Abraham onto the shelf, Jacob watched the image of the two members of their family's foundation now become complete. The grandmother he never met had her husband beside her again. His grandfather, his foundation, now lay silent in the cave of death. The ground under Jacob's feet felt unsteady.

The brothers wept as they stared at their father's body.

Jacob dared a peek at Esau who stood slightly stooped under the cave ceiling. Would the two of them mourn together when it was their father's time to pass on?

His gaze drifted around the chamber. Who would weep for him when it was his day to join the others in this burial cave? Who would he lay beside? His gaze fell to his mother. When would they have to bury her?

His empty heart squeezed. Death seemed to bring with it thoughts of more death. Was there anything that made life worth living if every person's life ended the same?

Rebekah's lips moved with silent words.

A smile pulled at the side of Jacob's mouth. He'd seen her do that enough to know. She was praying. Of course, she was praying.

He closed his eyes and imagined her words traveling out of the cave and up into the ears of Elohim. Would He be listening today? If the one He spoke to was dead, would He find someone else to speak to? Would the person be able to hear and understand as Abraham had?

Isaac's sudden movement caught Jacob's attention. He bowed to Ishmael. "Brother, I've called for you so that you could take your place as patriarch of Abraham's line."

Ishmael angled his head. His gaze took in the small gathering of them in the cave. He shook his head and put a hand on Isaac's shoulder. "No. It belongs to you."

Isaac opened his mouth to speak, but then snapped it shut. He pleaded softly, "It's yours. You are firstborn of Abraham, entitled to a double portion, and to lead this people."

Ishmael kept his eyes on his brother's face. "As tempting as it sounds, it's not my place. I may have sprung from Abraham's loins first, but Elohim chose you. It's not right for the son of a slave to take what belongs to the true son."

"But that's why I brought you here—"

Ishmael put his free hand up to stop him and then put the hand on Isaac's other shoulder to turn him so the two men were face to face. "It never belonged to me. It's always been waiting for you to claim it. You've waited seventy-five harvests, take hold of what is yours. May Elohim bless you richly, Brother." He smiled. "He already has done so for me."

"But I—"

"Besides." He released his grip and smacked his brother's arm. "I wouldn't know what to do with a bunch of sheep." He let a grin slip across his lips. "And I much prefer my spacious villa to a smelly ram-skinned tent." He winked, adding humor to the jab.

Isaac practically leapt into the arms of his brother and they joined in another round of wailing on behalf of their father.

Rebekah leaned on Jacob's arm; her gaze fixed on the two wrapped bodies. Soft tears streamed down her dusty cheeks. "Isn't it wonderful?"

Jacob took in the sight of his father and uncle's sorrow-filled joy.

She looked up at him. "The God, whose voice Abraham only heard, is now looking at him face to face."

Jacob returned his sight to the bodies. What did

Elohim have to say to his grandfather? What would He say when it was Jacob's turn to stand before Him?

Chapter 8

"Jacob said, 'Sell me your birthright now.' Esau said, 'I am about to die; of what use is a birthright to me?'"
-Genesis 25:31-32

Beerlahairoi, 1985 B.C.

Jacob's tongue stuck to the roof of his mouth. His throat burned to be quenched with fresh water. It was his choice to use the last drops from his waterskin to boil the wild red lentils he happened upon at sunrise. He should have drunk the water while he searched for more but, in a drought, it was an opportunity not to be missed.

His flock had been able to feast on a small patch of dew-covered grass Jacob found before the sun rose.

His flock. It felt good to finally be head over a flock of his own. With his grandfather's passing five harvests before, his father had his thriving flocks magnified with the acquisition of Abraham's riches. People, flocks, and possessions which were once under the control of Abraham, now belonged mostly to Isaac. Of course, there were provisions made for Abraham's six sons from Keturah, but Isaac received his double portion as the first legitimate born son.

Jacob looked over his tiny portion of his father's blessing. One day, when his father passed, most of the vast riches would not belong to him. Being second-born meant he would receive a smaller portion of his father's wealth. His older brother, Esau would gain what he had not worked for with his hands. Jacob's hard work managing his father's flocks would one day be handed over to his boulder-headed brother.

His chest tightened and he pushed away thoughts of the future. Esau was far away on another hunting trip. With each passing harvest, Esau stayed away longer. That was fine with Jacob, the more Esau was away, the longer between their scuffles and fights. Jacob's world was at peace among his flock and absent of his brother's constant goading.

The sheep and goats laid down in the little morning shade they could find. Jacob's diligent searching had paid off. They had their bellies filled. He stirred the small pot of stew. Now he was getting ready to fill his with the meager meal.

With the last measure of flour and oil, he mixed a single dough ball and threw it onto the flat rock he had warming over half the fire.

A breeze picked up the delicious aroma emanating

from the pot.

Out in the wilderness, he was not afforded the spices and herbs found in his mother's tent. Rebekah could turn any meal into a feast. Her hands moved like a dance each time she prepared food.

Jacob missed her lentil and vegetable stew. When they brought their flocks closer to home, a large bowl would be waiting for him each day with a stack of fresh bread as tall as his throwing rod neatly wrapped beside it. He missed the warmth of home. He missed his mother.

A dried bush beside him cracked with movement. He rose from his cooking fire with staff in hand. If a predator wanted to feed on his flock, he would be in for a fight.

A hairy man emerged and straightened to his full height. "Brother."

Jacob's empty stomach rolled. "Esau." He knelt back down.

The older twin came closer. His nostrils flared wildly as he sniffed the air. "That smells real good." He threw his bow over his head to settle it across his chest.

Jacob watched the arrows in the pack on his brother's back roll with the movement. Between the full quiver, empty arms, and the loud grumbles coming from his brother's stomach, he was sure the hunter had been unsuccessful in his latest trip.

Esau's large steps brought him even closer to the cooking fire. He leaned over almost dumping himself into the flames.

Jacob leapt to press against his bulky frame, but couldn't move the mountain back. "Watch out!"

Esau rocked back onto his heels. He swayed and then plopped himself beside the fire. His hand flew to his stomach and he rubbed it hard.

Jacob settled next to the flames, but kept his side glance on his brother. He flipped the bread to cook the other side.

Esau bent over. "Say, how about sharing some of that with me?"

"There isn't enough to share." Jacob stirred the stew. "There is barely enough to sustain myself."

"Come now, brother." Esau's stomach complained along with him. "Share with me."

He looked up into the mournful gaze of his brother. A wild idea crossed his mind. The crazy, unimaginable plan circled and circled until it consumed Jacob. His brother was perhaps just simple enough to fall into the trap. "No."

"Brother," Esau whined, "give me some of your stew or else I fear I may die."

"I will sell it to you."

Esau cringed. "I have nothing to barter with."

Jacob fought the smile that threatened to give away his plotting. The skilled hunter was moving ever closer into the trap Jacob was preparing for him. "But you do, Brother." His eyes moved from his stew to fully set on his pitiful twin. "Sell me your birthright."

His shoulders hung lower; his head fell forward with them. "If I die of hunger, what good is a birthright?"

"In an oath. Give me your birthright today by oath and I will give you my stew."

Esau lifted his gaze just enough to meet Jacob's. "I concede. My birthright as firstborn for your meal."

Jacob almost laughed as the trap closed around his unwitting brother. With exaggerated movements, he removed the pot from the fire and placed it before his brother's feet. The lentils hadn't even had time to soften, leaving the unfinished stew with a reddish appearance. It seemed almost laughable to serve the red stew to his red hair-covered brother. How fitting.

Esau moved to grab the pot.

"Wait." Jacob put his hand on top of the container. "Wouldn't you like some bread to go with it?" He pointed to the rock.

Esau's head bobbed.

With his stirring stick, Jacob removed the single flat loaf and wedged it into the pot.

"Is our oath complete?"

Jacob leaned back and gave a sharp nod. "You may enjoy your stew now."

With a movement almost too quick to see, Esau scooped up the bowl and lifted it to his lips. He used the bread to push the entire contents into his open mouth and then tossed the bread in after.

Jacob watched a line of stew drizzle out of the side

of his brother's enlarged mouth.

Esau chewed and chewed until nothing was left. He wiped the escaping drip with his thumb and then licked it clean. When he was done, he handed the empty pot to Jacob.

Jacob set the pot down. "Satisfied?"

Esau rose and rubbed his full stomach. "Thank you, Brother." He turned on his heels and disappeared back into the brush.

"No, Brother," he whispered to himself. "Thank you."

Weeks later, Jacob came upon his father.

Isaac stood with several other of his shepherds. He reached for his son. "I'm so glad you've come back this way, I was getting ready to send for you."

"Is everything well?"

"I'm afraid not." He shook his head. "This drought seems to have no end. I fear for our increased flocks and those who care for them. I think it's time we move."

"Further into the wilderness?"

"I mean away from Beerlahairoi."

"Leave our home?"

Isaac put a hand on his son's shoulders. "I know we've made it home for a long time." His thoughts drifted. "Your mother is certainly not going to be happy either, but I feel it best if we are going to outlast this drought."

"Where will we go?"

"North-east, toward Gerar. We've received word the land there is still lush and there is room enough for us all." He looked over the others. "We need to raise our stakes and move before we lose any to this dry land."

"Of course, *Abba.*"

Isaac smiled. "Thank you, son."

Jacob called for his flocks to follow and herded them back to the tent city they occupied during the cool months.

With time, the massive caravan of people moved from Beerlahairoi to the city of Gerar.

Jacob laid eyes on the lush fields ahead. He had almost forgotten what the colors of prosperity looked like.

Unfortunately, Esau had returned home from his hunting trip in time to move with the family. Jacob would have preferred the move without him.

Isaac halted the group. "Stay here," he called over his shoulder. "My family and I are going to see the king." He nodded to Rebekah and then to the boys.

Jacob set his pack down in the wagon and followed behind his mother.

The small family entered the city and made their way to the grand palace to seek an audience with the Philistine ruler.

The king granted their request. "So, this is the famed son of Abraham." He waved toward Isaac. "Please come closer."

Isaac bowed, motioning for the rest to follow.

Jacob dipped his head and fell in line behind his parents.

"That's better." He eased back into his throne. "Tell me, Isaac, what brings you to my city?"

"If you'll oblige us, great king, there has come a great famine in our land. One greater than even my *abba* saw in all his years. I have been set to care for the mass of people and animals my *abba* left behind. Your *abba* made an oath of peace with mine in Beersheba. If it pleases your greatness, my family and I would like to have your permission to live here in order to survive this plague."

Jacob watched the king's eyes travel all over his mother's form. His stomach turned watching the man openly admire his mother.

"You may stay." The king feigned interest. "But tell me, who is this lovely creature you've brought with you?"

Isaac glanced at Rebekah. His lips parted, then snapped shut. He turned his attention back to the king. "She is my sister, your greatness."

"Sister?" He wet his lips. "My, she is beautiful."

"Yes," Isaac swallowed hard, "she is very beautiful indeed."

The king straightened. "Your people may stay in the city and there is plenty of surrounding land to feed your livestock."

"May Elohim bless your kindness, king."

He nodded, but kept his eyes on Rebekah.

Isaac backed out of the room motioning for his family to follow.

As soon as the gate to the palace was firmly shut behind them, Rebekah turned on her husband. "Why did you tell him I was your sister?"

Isaac moved her further down the street with quick glances over his shoulder. "I had to." He kept his gaze on the people around them. "Did you see the way he was watching you?"

She shook her head.

"You don't see the way the men here stare?" He motioned with his chin.

Rebekah glanced around them. "So? Why not tell him I was your wife and settle the matter?"

"The matter would only be settled with my death. Is that what you want!"

Rebekah shrunk at his rising tone.

Isaac pushed his hair back. "Forgive me. I didn't mean to shout." He pulled her close. "If I had told the king you were my wife, these men would have killed me for you. If I claim you as my sister, at least they might try to make an offer for you that I can simply refuse. It keeps both our necks attached to our heads."

Rebekah rubbed her throat. "I see."

Jacob felt the heat rise in his own throat. What kind of people had his father brought them to live among? Could they really have peace in this city?

Chapter 9

*"When he had been there a long time, Abimelech
king of the Philistines looked out of a window and
saw Isaac laughing with Rebekah his wife."
-Genesis 26:8*

Rebekah

Rebekah stretched her aching back. The past few
weeks of arranging a new home wore her old bones.
Hadiya and Deborah helped, but both had gone to aid
others in the tent city and gave Rebekah some much-
needed time with her husband. He had been away
more in their marriage than with her.

She looked around at all her work. Living in a tent
seemed much easier than setting up life in the city of
Gerar. Had it really been so long ago that she lived in
a home made of stone instead of ram skins?

The small two-story dwelling the king had given to
them sat next to the palace. It was simple, but more

than they needed.

She reached to unpack the last basket. Inside she discovered one of Jacob's tunics. Rubbing the worn material in her fingers she thought about her son laying in the fields with the flocks. He much preferred tents and sheep to stone homes and people. She smiled. He was so much like her.

Thoughts drifted to Esau next. Where would his hunting take him this time? He barely slept one night under their new roof before he was off claiming that a new land meant new opportunities to hunt.

Without Jacob and Esau, the new home felt empty.

Movement on the roof grabbed her attention and she climbed the simple ladder to ascend to the rooftop.

Isaac paced.

She made her way to him and hugged him tight. "What troubles you?"

He held her to arm's length and sighed. "I've been praying to Elohim."

"Something's happened?" She searched his face trying to discover the answer there.

"I received word from Ishmael. He heard of the famine in Beerlahairoi and offered for us to join him closer to Egypt."

"You've always wanted to be closer to your brother. I'm sure his connections there would bless us."

"I'm sure they would too." He looked toward the fading light of day.

Rebekah held onto him. "But?"

Isaac turned back to her. "But last night I had a dream. Elohim spoke to me, warning me not to go to Egypt. He reminded me of the oath He swore to my *abba* and the promise to bless us."

"If Elohim said no, I think we should listen."

"Me too." He caressed her cheek. "Me too."

"Then we shall remain here in Gerar until Elohim tells us to leave."

He pulled her in close and smiled. "We shall." His lips found hers as the first star peeked out overhead.

Rebekah laid her head on Isaac's chest. His heart beat wildly under her ear. "Is that all that troubles you, my husband?"

He took a deep breath and let it out slowly. He rubbed his cheek against the top of her head. "I miss my flock."

"Me too." She giggled. "I'm sure Jacob and Jedidiah have them well in hand."

"I know." He hugged her one last time and then pulled away. "I just wish I were out there too."

She reached for his arm. "Well, in the morning we can find you something to do, but for tonight..." She traced her fingers up his arm.

His smile broadened. "Why Elohim chose to bless me with such a woman as you, I'll never know."

"Then you should show how thankful you are."

He intertwined their fingers and led her to the ladder.

When Rebekah's foot found solid ground, a rough knock came at the door.

Isaac looked at her.

"I'm not expecting anyone."

He moved to open the door.

Two guards filled the small doorway. "Isaac, son of Abraham?"

Isaac straightened his shoulders. "I am he."

"Your presence is requested before the king along with your..." the guard looked over Isaac's shoulder to Rebekah, "...sister."

"Of course." He motioned for Rebekah to follow them out.

The two hurried behind the marching feet in front of them.

Rebekah pulled her headwrap up and tight around her face. The cool of evening chilled her tired bones.

The guards led them through the palace gates and into the large chamber where the king heard from his people.

Atop the throne sat the king. His face pulled taut as if he had sucked on sour grapes. His body was rigid as if poised to strike an enemy.

Rebekah gulped and stuck close to Isaac.

When they were a respectful distance away, Isaac stopped and bowed.

Rebekah followed his movements.

"Guards, you are dismissed."

Rebekah watched the two men exchange a quick

uncertain glance before obeying.

The king waited until the room emptied before he spoke. "Isaac. Son of Abraham. The woman who stands beside you is your wife."

Rebekah swallowed hard, but kept her eyes on the tiled floor. She didn't need to look at the king's face to recognize his anger. It was clear in his voice.

"Why then did you tell me she was your sister?"

Isaac fell to his knees. "I feared for my life, your greatness." His forehead smacked the tile. "If I admitted she was my wife, I feared I would be killed for her."

Rebekah knelt hard. The cold tile hitting her knees sent a sting of pain and chill up her body.

"Why have you done this to my people? One of them might have lain with your wife and brought guilt upon us all."

Isaac quaked.

Rebekah counted heartbeats.

"Guards!"

Rebekah's chest tightened, she gasped quietly for breath. This was it. The king's mercy toward them would end this night, but would it end with their bodies intact. Images of Jacob standing peacefully in the field among his father's flocks was the thought she clung to as death crept upon them with marching sandals slapping against tile.

When the sound of footsteps ceased, Rebekah looked to see the soldier's feet beside her.

"Make it known throughout the land," the king's voice boomed in the large room. "No one is to touch this man or his wife. If anyone touches either one of them, that person will be put to death."

Rebekah couldn't believe her ears. The king wasn't ordering their deaths. He was adding protection to them.

"Thank you, your greatness," Isaac's voice trembled as he rose from the ground.

Rebekah lifted on shaking legs, but dared not a glance at the ruler.

"I have more to say to you, son of Abraham."

Isaac bowed his head.

"Though I have spared your life this night and henceforth, I do think it best you take your wife and go live in the valley. To remove temptation, you see." He took a breath. "A king's order can't remove the beauty from your wife's face and I don't wish to sacrifice my people on the altar of her loveliness."

"I understand." Isaac bowed in half. "It will be as you have requested."

"Good." He leaned back. "And one more thing."

Isaac waited.

"Try not to follow so closely in your father's footsteps. You might find yourself where you don't wish to be."

Curiosity got the better of Rebekah and she peered up at the king through the veil of her fallen hair.

His gaze was transfixed on her.

She moved her glance to her husband.

"Thank you again, your greatness." Isaac motioned for Rebekah to take a step back. "With your permission, we shall take our leave. We have packing to do."

The king waved his hand.

Isaac grabbed Rebekah's arm and nearly dragged her from the room.

He was quiet until they made it all the way to the house and behind the latched door. He leaned on the door with both hands. "Forgive my deceit. I fear I might have placed us in more danger with it than what I had imagined with the truth." He turned toward her.

Rebekah stood shaking in the center of the room. "What did the king mean about your *abba*?"

Isaac shook his head and ran his fingers through his damp hair. "That's where I got the idea. My *abba* stood before the previous king and even Pharaoh before that. He saw the hunger lust in all those men's eyes for my *ima*. Abraham lied...well half lied about her. He claimed her to be his sister, but left out the part about them being man and wife also. She was the daughter of his *abba* Terah, but not by the same mother. I figured I could succeed where my *abba* failed."

"Failed?"

"Each time the rulers found out about the deception it was because Elohim had brought a plague on their land."

"Isaac!"

"I know." He tucked his head. "But I had to take the risk. I couldn't lose you to another man."

She rushed to him and wept. "I'm so sorry. It's all my fault."

Isaac placed a light palm on her cheek and rubbed her tears away. "You've never seen how truly beautiful you are, my love." His eyes lit up his smile. "Your beauty is illuminated by Elohim's breath in you. Just like Eve." He winked.

"Oh, Isaac." She collapsed into his arms. "I'm so glad we are going back to our tents."

"Me too, beloved." He brushed her hair.

Rebekah held on tight. Soon she would be back under the stars Elohim dotted His sky with and the sheep He had given them. Her family would be whole again in the ever-expanding tent city she called home.

The end of their very first harvest produced an abundance in the valley of Gerar.

Rebekah watched pride refresh her husband. Elohim was blessing them and it only confirmed their choice to stay.

But the joy that filled their hearts would soon come under attack. After years of living in the valley at peace with their Philistine neighbors, jealousy reached new heights. Each day, Isaac came home to report another one of the wells he had dug had been stopped up by

Philistine shepherds. He spent his days settling disputes only to have to resettle them again the next. With each new fight, they packed up their tents and moved further south.

Rebekah noticed Isaac's stance droop more and more each night he came to eat his last meal of the day with her. She tried everything she could to cheer him, but the responsibility of managing such a large group of people and animals weighed heavily on the patriarch's shoulders.

After pitching their tents in Beersheba, Isaac sat outside watching the sunrise over the fields.

Rebekah sat next to him. "How long do you think we can stay here?"

"I don't know." He sighed. "But I know that no matter where we stake our tent spikes, Elohim will be faithful to us."

She shook her head. "I don't understand any of this. I thought the king's order would help protect us."

"His order was that no man touch us. He didn't tell them they couldn't impede our prosperity."

"But they haven't. Elohim has made sure of that."

Isaac pulled her close to himself. "Yes, He has." He put his chin on her head. "Do you know I dreamed that He spoke to me last night?"

Rebekah pulled back to look him in the face. "Tell me about it. I've so missed His voice in my dreams."

"Well, Elohim appeared to me and said, 'I am the God of Abraham your father. Fear not, for I am with you and will bless you and multiply your offspring for my servant Abraham's sake.' "

"You see. No matter what these Philistines try to do to us, Elohim will still bless us because of your *abba's* faithfulness and yours."

He smiled. "I knew there was a reason I loved you." His face brightened. "Do you know what I want to do here?"

She tilted her head. "What?"

"I want to build an altar. We haven't had a family altar since leaving Beerlahairoi."

"Oh yes." She clapped her hands. "Let's."

The next day was spent building a new altar.

By the time the sun was past the halfway point in the sky, Rebekah stood beside the place they would lay their offerings to Elohim.

Isaac stood rubbing the flat stone. Then his attention caught over Rebekah's head.

She turned to see what he was watching.

Dust kicked up along the far path. She couldn't make out much except that the sun's light reflected off armor. *Soldiers.* She clung to Isaac. "What do you think they want?"

"I don't know." He squinted into the brightness. "But they are wearing the king's colors. They are royal guards."

Before Rebekah could think of what to do next, they were descended upon by the approaching sentinels.

The king, flanked by two men and a small host of his guard came toward them. "Isaac, son of Abraham, and his lovely wife, Rebekah." He waved his arms wide as if he were going to embrace them.

Isaac and Rebekah bowed deeply.

"May I present my adviser, Ahuzzath, and the commander of my army, Phicol."

The couple bowed to the men behind the king.

Isaac spoke for them, "What have we done to invite the honor of his greatness to join us in the fields? I have taken my leave of your valley since I believed you hated me."

"Hate?" He waved him off. "Come now, Isaac. I do not hold any hate for you. We have seen plainly that your God has been with you. So, having spoken with my advisor, I decided to come to offer you a covenant. That you will do us no harm, just as we have not touched you and have done nothing but good to your people. You are truly blessed of Elohim."

Rebekah wanted greatly to argue the fact that they've had to move so many times because, in fact, the king's people have shown nothing but contempt for her family. She knew better than to part her lips in such matters. At least the king was trying to offer peace, even if his roaming eyes couldn't seem to find their way from her form.

Isaac bowed in half. "Then let us feast together and bind our agreement."

"Wonderful." The king ordered his men to make

room.

"Spread word," Isaac whispered in Rebekah's ear. "Have any free hands help prepare a grand meal."

She nodded and rushed to obey.

With the many hands among their tent city, food appeared as if rained down from the sky itself. They spent the rest of the day eating, drinking, and sharing stories over the feast before them.

When the oath was bound between the king and Isaac, the royal host departed the fields.

Rebekah watched the group march away. *Peace.* Her heart nearly sang the word. Would it be sure now among her people?

"Isaac!" Jedidiah rushed towards them. "We've found water!"

Rebekah turned to her husband. "What are you going to call this well?"

He pulled at his beard for several moments before the name flowed over his lips, "Shibah."

She smiled. *An oath.* The king's oath would provide protection, but Elohim's oath to them had been renewed and confirmed again. That's all she needed.

Chapter 10

*"When Esau was forty years old, he took Judith the
daughter of Beeri the Hittite to be his wife, and
Basemath the daughter of Elon the Hittite, and they
made life bitter for Isaac and Rebekah."*
-Genesis 26:34-35

Beersheba, 1965 B.C.

Rebekah ground heads of barley in the crisp air outside
her tent. She inhaled the refreshing breeze that
brought peace to her soul and cooled the ferocity of the
final days of scorching heat. This was her favorite time
of year. Of course, the warmth she felt for the change
of weather was only flamed with images of her
shepherd husband and son coming back to camp under
her tent for the next few months.

As the evenings lengthened, she enjoyed spending
more time outside preparing meals and treats while she
listened to the children of the camp play between the

tents. The dogs too old to keep up with the flocks took turns on sentinel duty keeping the young ones close and enemies away.

Zelpha, one of the oldest females who had produced her fair share of quality litters, strolled over and slumped beside Rebekah.

A smile eased over her lips as she reached to pet the old Kangal. "We are both not as young as we think we are, huh?"

With a heavy pant, the dog pressed into her caresses.

She lifted a piece of old bread toward her.

Zelpha accepted the simple treat.

Rebekah watched several children run by. "It must be tough to keep up with all those young bodies."

The dog hoisted herself back onto all fours and marched after her fleeing flock.

"Keep a good eye on them, mighty *ima*." She picked up her stone pestle and returned to her grinding.

Hadiya came out of the tent beside her. "Shouldn't the men be returning soon?"

Rebekah closed her eyes and breathed in the cool air again. "I'm hoping today." She opened her eyes to meet the curious glance of her handmaid. "It's when I would come in."

She moved to kneel beside her. "Do you miss the wilderness?"

"Oh, very much." Rebekah rubbed the fresh

grounds into a fine powder. "Sleeping in an open field surrounded by a flock with nothing but time to think and a good dog beside you, nothing beats that."

Hadiya raised an eyebrow.

"Of course, I love the life Elohim has given me. Two strong boys, an ever-expanding camp of people I adore," she reached an arm around her handmaid and pulled her close, "and two of the best companions I could ask for."

She chuckled.

Deborah appeared beside them. "I hope none of that gossip is about me." She put a hand on her broad hip, but a smile danced at her lips.

Rebekah reached for her.

The old nurse nestled by her other side.

"I was just telling Hadiya how thankful I was for the life we share."

Deborah huffed. "I for one would be a lot happier if we had some grandchildren around this tent. I'm not getting younger."

Another group of children ran by laughing.

Rebekah waved toward them. "Are there not plenty of children around here for you to scold?"

Deborah swatted playfully at her.

Rebekah wrapped her arms around the older woman's neck and kissed her cheek. "I only jest. Any child would be blessed to lay at your chest or sit at your feet."

Deborah set her chin on top of Rebekah's head. "I

don't know if I will make it to see your bright eyes shine from another young one."

Rebekah sighed and straightened. "The boys have already seen their fortieth harvest. I don't know why Isaac has waited so long."

Hadiya spoke up, "Didn't you say Isaac himself had seen forty harvests when you became his wife?"

"Yes."

"Perhaps he is hoping the boys will follow in his footsteps and wait for such a bride as you."

Rebekah moved to lay her head on her handmaid's shoulder. "You always know just how to turn a situation toward the sun, Hadiya." She sighed. "But it will be years before Laban's daughters come of age."

The three women sat watching the flames of the cooking fire dance.

Rebekah added oil to the barley flour and mixed it together. Once satisfied, she threw the lump onto the hot, flat rock and spread it flat. She poked at the loaf until it began to steam. Then she flipped it.

As the sun touched the horizon, two figures appeared at the crest of the hill. With the sun to their backs, their faces were veiled in darkness, but Rebekah knew those two forms better than she knew her own body. She handed her cooking stick to Hadiya and rushed toward them.

Practically leaping into her husband's arms, her momentum caused them to twirl. She kissed his right cheek, then his left, then his right again. "It makes my heart soar to see you, my husband."

Isaac tightened his grip on her. "I'm happy to see you are well, beloved."

Rebekah released her grip only enough to pull Jacob in. "My son has returned! We shall feast your arrival."

Jacob attempted to hide the smile that warmed his expression.

Isaac tensed.

Rebekah felt his movement and held them both out.

The two men exchanged a look of uncertainty.

Rebekah studied both of their faces. "What?"

"I'll let *Abba* tell you." Jacob kissed his mother's cheek and headed toward the tent.

She turned to her husband and raised an eyebrow. "Tell me what?"

He sighed and wiped the hair out of his face. "We ran into Esau on the trip back."

"Esau?" Rebekah's heart galloped. Her other son spent more time away from her tent than her shepherds. It had been many months since she last saw him. "Is he well?"

"He is well. Bigger than any man I've met. I don't think that boy will ever stop growing." He chuckled softly.

"And?"

"And…" he cleared his throat, "it seems during these last months away he has taken wives."

"Wives?" The word sent shivers down Rebekah's back. "What does that mean?"

"We met him to pass along the news of the agreement we made with Laban to betroth our sons to his daughters. But he felt I had kept the right of a wife from him too long and decided to take the responsibility upon himself." Isaac closed his eyes. "Apparently, one was not enough for him and so he took a second as soon as the first's marriage week was complete." He opened his eyes to study her.

Rebekah clenched her fists beside her legs and then released them.

"Rebekah? Say something."

"How could he?"

"I know it's not our hope for him but—"

"You don't understand." She shook her head. "We've already sent word to Laban about the betrothals. What are we going to do now?"

He pulled her in close and put his cheek on her forehead. "I don't know."

"Should we send word to my brother?"

He was silent for several heartbeats.

"Isaac?"

"I don't know, beloved." He held her out. "I simply don't know what to do. Maybe Esau will be open to still marrying Laban's oldest?"

"Isaac! How can you wish such a thing on our niece? She was supposed to be the first and only wife to our oldest? And now? Now what? She might have the chance to be a third wife?"

"It's better than not being a wife at all."

She smacked at his chest and pulled away. "I can't believe your words. This is your fault. If you had chosen brides for them before now, Esau wouldn't have chosen his own."

He stepped toward her. "Remember, beloved, it was your idea to wait and see if Laban produced girls. It is not my fault it took him so long. He even took a concubine to wife with your expectation hanging over his head. But she produced only sons. It will still be years before Laban's daughters can be given to our sons. Did you honestly expect them to wait forever?"

"You always do this," she felt the taste of venomous words sting her tongue, but she released them like poisoned arrows anyway. "Your beloved Esau can do no wrong. Even after he leaves you and Jacob to work the flocks and runs to hunt instead. Even after he stays away for months on end filling his stomach instead of working his hands to expand your wealth. All because he brings you prized pieces of his game to fill your own stomach. Even now as he has usurped your role and taken not one but two wives for himself." She waved two of her fingers in his face before realization dawned on her. "Canaanites?"

He flinched and dropped his head. "Hittites."

"Hittites?" She put her hands over her mouth and squinted at him.

His look pleaded for her to cease, but he said no

more.

She turned on her sandaled heels and ducked into her tent.

Jacob rummaged through one of his baskets.

She stood in the main area trying to slow her racing heart and breath.

Jacob rose and moved toward her. "So, he told you about Esau?"

She closed her eyes and nodded.

"Did he tell you all of it?"

Her eyes popped open and she stared at him.

Jacob folded. "Esau is bringing them here." He took a breath and held his hands up to her. "To live here with you while he returns to hunt."

Rebekah felt the heat rise from her chest, push past her cheeks, and catch into fire in her eyes.

Jacob took a step back. "I told *Abba* it wasn't a good idea, but he insisted."

She felt the heat surge and work its way up into her hairline to the point she could probably finish cooking bread on her forehead. "Isaac insisted?"

He nodded while taking another step backward. His back almost touched the tent wall. "*Abba* said it might be good for them to live here so you could get to know them better."

"I don't want to get to know those idol worshippers better." She folded her arms.

"I think he's hoping you'll win them to Elohim as he did you."

"Those heathens are too far gone to be reached. You don't know the vile things they do."

Jacob pulled at his short beard. "Would someone have said that about you, *Ima*?"

Her breath caught and her gaze fell to the carpets. "I don't know what you're talking about."

"*Abba* told me about your life in Padanaram before you became his bride." He took a slight step closer to her. "Before you came to Elohim."

She sighed and lifted her chin. "Some might have thought me too far, yes."

"Then give them a chance too." He reached for her. "Give Elohim a chance."

She smiled a half-smile and reached her hand to fill his. "You're right. Forgive me."

He pulled her in for an embrace. "Elohim has a bigger plan than we know, *Ima*. Let's work on trusting Him together."

Rebekah closed her eyes and listened to the strong heartbeat of her youngest son. She inhaled the smell of fresh air, open fields, and animals that mingled with his sweat. Her boy wasn't a boy anymore. Somewhere in the fields among the flocks, he had become a man. One rooted in Elohim.

Strange voices from outside the tent caught her attention. She looked up into Jacob's worn and twisted face.

"Did I forget to mention that they were right behind us?"

Rebekah pulled back. "Today? They are arriving today?"

He nodded and put a soft hand on her shoulder. "Remember to trust Elohim."

She took a deep breath. "Trust Elohim." She nodded and inhaled again. "Trust Elohim." The words became a soft chant under her breath as she moved to exit the tent.

When she pressed back the tent flap, Esau stood at least two heads above his father. He had not stopped growing. His shoulder spread wide as if they were attempting to escape one another. His skin was tanned by many days catching game and his lack of clothing to cover most of it.

Two women stood with him, one on either side. They too wore little to cover themselves and what threads did hang off their bodies were tied with precious metals and jewels. Their yellowish skin stuck out against Esau's olive complexion.

"Rebekah." Isaac summoned her with a wave. "Come meet our daughters-in-law."

She took a shaky step toward them, repeating her chant silently to herself.

"*Ima.*" Esau brightened at her approach. "I would like you to meet my wives, Aholibamah and Adah." He motioned to each woman.

Rebekah bowed.

The woman on Esau's left turned toward him. "I don't understand why you insist on changing our names. I like the name my father chose, Judith, much better."

"I like mine too, Bashemath."

Esau hushed the women. "You will be called what I have declared and no other. You now belong to me, and I will call you what I wish."

Rebekah felt her heart squeeze. Perhaps Jacob was right. These women needed to know the kindness of Elohim. They had been taken from their homes to live in the wilderness among strangers. Certainly, she should do what she could to make them feel welcomed.

"The evening meal is almost ready." Rebekah waved to Deborah and Hadiya who had taken over for her. "Won't you join us?"

The girls turned hungry eyes on their husband.

"We shall eat."

"But first," Rebekah held up a finger, "I think it best we find some...acceptable clothes."

Esau looked down at his loincloth and then to his wives' wraps. "If it will make you happy, *Ima*."

"It would." She waved to Hadiya. "My handmaid can find some dresses for the girls."

Esau pressed the two women toward the tent.

Jacob neared Rebekah to whisper in her ear, "Thank you, *Ima*." He exhaled slowly. "I don't know if I could have kept my gaze on the fire all night."

She reached up to cup his cheek. "Promise me something, my son."

"Anything, *Ima*."

She held his steady gaze. "Promise me you will never marry a Canaanite woman."

"I promise." He moved his lips to kiss her palm.

"Good boy." She brushed his thick beard. "Now, let us enjoy a good meal together, and you can tell me about your time in the wilderness."

She allowed him to lead the way to the fire. Her thoughts drifted to her far-away nieces. One of those infant girls didn't know it yet, but if Rebekah had anything to do with it, she would one day hold the heart of an amazing man. If only Esau had waited too.

Chapter 11

"These are the years of the life of Ishmael: 137 years. He breathed his last and died, and was gathered to his people."
-Genesis 25:17

Kedesh, 1941 B.C.

Rebekah stood outside a great cave with Isaac on one side and Jacob on the other. Isaac's soft whimpers reverberated through her. His dear older brother Ishmael had breathed his last.

They received word from his wife for them to attend the burial. She thought it only right for Isaac to be there as it was his brother's dying wish. Ishmael had wanted to send word of his illness earlier, but thought he would recover. He was wrong and made her promise to only gather him to his people with Isaac in attendance.

Rebekah felt her body tremble under the grief of her husband.

Jacob slid his hand around hers and squeezed. A gentle reminder of his calming presence and their constant choice to trust Elohim.

She squeezed back.

Isaac moved toward the wrapped body of his brother.

Rebekah's gaze flowed over the massive gathering surrounding them. It nearly rivaled the one for Abraham.

Ishmael's sons and daughters along with their extended families circled them. Half of Egypt was present along with some members of Isaac's camp.

Esau had been gone on another hunt and his wives had elected to stay behind in Beersheba instead of traveling to Kedesh. Deborah offered to stay with the women to keep them out of trouble. Hadiya stood behind Rebekah. Another source of quiet strength.

The burial process was long and full of all the nobility Ishmael deserved. He was Abraham's firstborn, though not heir. Elohim had seen fit to bless him anyway because of the sincere cries of a slave woman. Their Creator certainly liked to do things His own way.

By the time Ishmael lay among his people and Rebekah and her family returned home, they were all tired not just in body, but also of spirit.

Isaac retreated to his tent, choosing to stay behind instead of going with Jacob and the other shepherds to care for the flocks. Rebekah couldn't blame him. He had lost his older sibling, and his body had seen over one hundred and twenty harvests. If anyone deserved a reprieve, it was him.

The next morning, Rebekah woke to the sounds of screams. She shook her head trying to push whatever nightmare gripped her from her sleep. The sounds of Isaac's wails brought her upright and out of the tent. She tripped over tent stakes in the dim morning light.

Isaac stumbled toward her clawing at his face.

Rebekah grasped his shoulders and forced him inside their tent. "Isaac? What has happened?"

He fumbled around still holding his face and screaming in pain.

She wrestled him to the ground. "Isaac? Please speak to me."

He thrashed.

"Hadiya!"

The handmaid rushed into the room from the other side of their tent. "What's wrong?"

"I'm not sure yet." Rebekah pressed on Isaac's shoulders trying to keep him still.

Hadiya knelt beside them. She put a hand on Isaac's arm. "Master Isaac, it's me, Hadiya. I need you to move your hands for just a moment."

He pulled away and wailed.

"Please don't fight me, Master. I need to see the extent of the damage."

Her words sent chills racing up and down Rebekah's back. She pulled her simple sleeping dress tighter against her body.

At her touch, Isaac's screams quieted into soft sobs. She tugged gently on his wrists until his hands slid down his face.

Rebekah gasped and turned around to hold her stomach. Though she had been awakened before breaking her fast, the queasiness that hit her threatened to bring forth anything it could find in her stomach. She swallowed hard and peeked over her shoulder.

Hadiya examined the injury.

Isaac's face which was once a beautiful, olive color was now mixed with blood and burns that were already blistering. His bright, dark eyes were transformed into two charred pits of emptiness.

Hadiya looked up at Rebekah and shook her head. She patted Isaac's hand and rose. She pushed Rebekah toward the tent flap and whispered, "We need to find out what happened. The damage can't be mended, but if we find out what burned him, we can get rid of it."

"What could cause such a burn?" She shook her head trying to lose an idea to explain her husband's injury. "We haven't even started the morning fire yet."

Hadiya looked over at Isaac. "Maybe he had gone for a walk and encountered something?"

The tent flap beside Rebekah lifted in the breeze bringing with it the distinct mixture of spices and fire. She knew that scent. A horrid smell she had endured for over twenty harvests. Her daughters-in-law's morning prayers to their gods included burning spices.

She pushed aside the flap and stepped outside. In the sands, a trail of blood led toward the north through the nearby tents. Her heart dropped as her gaze lifted to see the familiar smoke rising from Esau's tent. The women he called wives hadn't enjoyed living next to her and moved to the far edge of the tent city. Esau hadn't minded. He barely stayed under their goatskin long enough to notice or care what they did.

As she drew near, the faint sound of laughter floated toward her. Not the kind of laughter one heard from the lips of an old friend or the joyful sound of a child at play. This was a screeching noise Rebekah imagined would come from the throat of an enemy.

The blood in her body boiled. These women had injured her husband, their leader, and here they stood...laughing. She marched toward them.

Their fire burned large and discolored by whatever strange herbs and spices they had thrown into it. Bones and flesh mingled with the flames as the two women danced around the pit.

Rebekah came close enough to catch their attention. They stopped and stared at her. She watched fear crawl into their gaze. Without hesitating, she rushed them and grabbed for their flesh. The two slipped beyond her grasp. Rebekah chased them around the fire clawing at them.

She reached again and caught the thin wrap of Adah. With all her strength, she pulled the woman to her face and screamed, "Why?"

The woman tugged away. "Please don't hurt me. We meant no harm."

Aholibamah pulled Rebekah's arm. "Let her go. We truly didn't mean to hurt him."

Rebekah held her grasp. "Why?"

"He tried to stop our ceremony," Adah's voice trembled. "All we wanted to do was finish. He came near our tent yelling for us to stop. We tried to tell him we couldn't, but he just kept screaming at us."

"I had a bowl of our mixes and threw it into the flames." Aholibamah held her head. "He was standing too close to the fire, and it stood up to strike him in the face." Her knees gave way and she hit the sand hard. "I didn't want to hurt him; I was just trying to get him to stop yelling."

"Well, you succeeded." Rebekah dug her nails into Adah's flesh.

The girl cried out.

"Your fire has consumed my husband's face and I'm afraid his sight along with it."

Adah collapsed under Rebekah's hold. "If he had only left us, he would not have gotten hurt. Please don't harm us."

The two women shook at her feet.

"I should feed the two of you to your own strange fire." Her eyes flicked to the flames. Rustling from nearby tents produced glares from those peeking out to see what all the uproar was about. Looking into the faces of the people she held dear, her thoughts were of

Elohim. What would have become of her had He not reached into her life? "But…" she sighed and released Adah.

The girl scurried to Aholibamah's side and held onto her.

"But Elohim would have me forgive you as He has forgiven me." She lowered her shoulders and turned in the direction of her tent without a backward glance.

When she reached the tent, she pushed back the flap and entered.

Hadiya knelt in front of Isaac wrapping his head in a clean linen.

Jacob stood to the side and rushed toward Rebekah when she entered. "What happened?"

Rebekah looked past him to Hadiya.

"*Ima?*"

Her eyes met his. "Esau's wives."

Jacob's brows jumped up.

"He was burned by their strange fire." Tears threatened to take her voice.

Jacob's cheeks flamed. "Then I shall relieve my brother of these idol worshippers."

Rebekah grabbed his arm. "Trust Elohim."

He eased. "What did you say?"

"You taught me. Trust Elohim. Even when things don't look right. Trust."

Jacob shook his head.

"They need to see Him, Jacob. They need to know our God."

Jacob pulled her into his chest.

She stared at her husband's wrapped face and sobbed.

Hadiya stood and walked toward them. "He should rest. I'll check the bandage regularly, but I don't know what more I can do."

"Adah and Aholibamah," the names slipped from Rebekah's quivering lips. "They did this."

"With all the herbs they possess, there might be something among them that might aid his healing."

"Go." Rebekah rubbed her face in Jacob's tunic. "Check their supply and take whatever you think will help."

"You think they would freely give to me from their stock?"

"Tell them I gave you permission." She wiped her nose on the back of her sleeve. "They won't stop you."

Hadiya hesitated.

"Go!"

She dipped her head and was out of the tent faster than a flash of lightning.

Jacob rubbed Rebekah's back. "Don't be so hard on your handmaid, *Ima*. She's only trying to help."

"I know." She laid a cheek on his chest again. "Remind me to thank her when she returns."

He wrapped his arms around her. "Why don't I start some stew?"

Rebekah looked up at him.

"I'm sure *Abba* will be hungry."

"I'm sure he will be."

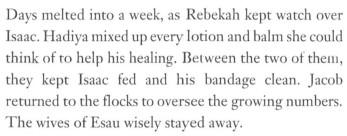

Days melted into a week, as Rebekah kept watch over Isaac. Hadiya mixed up every lotion and balm she could think of to help his healing. Between the two of them, they kept Isaac fed and his bandage clean. Jacob returned to the flocks to oversee the growing numbers. The wives of Esau wisely stayed away.

When the week was complete, Hadiya removed the bandage. "Master Isaac, can you tell me how many fingers I'm holding up?"

Isaac swayed back and forth in front of her.

Rebekah stared at the marred flesh that had begun to heal. Never again would he look upon her in that loving way he reserved for only her.

"No," Isaac whispered. "I see only darkness."

"Maybe a little longer." Rebekah put a hand on his. "We are going to step outside the tent for a moment, my husband."

He bowed his head.

Rebekah rose and motioned for Hadiya to follow her.

The women stood outside the tent.

Rebekah looked around to make sure they were alone. "Speak, Hadiya, or I shall pull the words out of your mouth myself."

She swallowed hard. "I've done all I can, Mistress. There has been much improvement in his skin.

Unfortunately, there is not an herb on land or in the sea that can possibly restore all that has been lost…"

Rebekah knew she didn't have to continue. She had known since she first saw the damage to her husband's face. The fire had claimed his eyes and his sight along with it. Nothing would return them. She nodded and turned to go back into the tent. Once inside, she knelt beside Isaac.

"Rebekah?"

"It is I." She wiped her face. "How did you know?"

"You love to rub olive oil into the cracks of your heels. I can smell it when you walk near."

She smiled as she took in the man sitting in her tent. Her sweet husband was still there. The man who had loved her from the moment he saw her was still there. Esau's wives' fire might have taken his sight, but it hadn't taken her husband.

"Oh, Isaac, I'm so sorry. I tried to tell you I did not trust those she-demons. Now look what they have done to you," she sobbed.

He reached toward her.

She bowed into his grip as he pulled her into his lap. His muscular arms wrapped around her. He rocked her back and forth as she had done for her sons when they had scraped a young knee. When his arms were tired, he released his hold on her.

She eased to his side. With her finger, she lightly traced the burn lines on his face. Starting at his forehead where a small patch of hair was missing, the burned skin there had healed the most. The hair above both his eyes was gone and the place where his eyes should have been were only empty pits. Her caress followed the marks down one cheek and under his eye, across his nose to the other side. As her finger traveled farther, the damage lessened. The space under his nose and above his top lip was burned, but his lips seemed only mildly injured. Her fingertips rested softly on his deep red and cracked lips.

He puckered them to kiss her fingers. "I'm still here, beloved."

"Where you belong, my husband." Tears fell freely down her face.

Her husband was there, but would never be the same. He would never see a sunrise over the abundance of flocks. Never see the mischief dance in her eyes when they were alone. He would not return to the fields. She felt a sting of relief. He would now be forced to stay in her tent for the rest of the days Elohim would give them. That was well with her. She would be his eyes. She would love him as she did when her eyes first laid on his handsome face.

She pressed away some of his unruly hair and kissed his cheek with a feather-light touch.

"*Abba?*" Jacob's voice called from outside the tent.

Isaac straightened. "Come forth."

Jacob ducked his head to enter. He stepped toward them and knelt before his father. "I brought you something."

Rebekah smiled an approving glance at him.

Jacob put a wrapped item in his father's lap.

Isaac felt it carefully. "What have you brought me, my son."

Rebekah put a hand over her husband's. "Let me help."

With their hands working together, they unwrapped the cloth.

Isaac's face searched for something he couldn't see. His hand rubbed up and down the unseen item in his lap.

"It's a new staff." Rebekah clapped. "It's beautiful."

"Carved it myself." Jacob beamed.

Isaac ran his fingers over the carved wood.

"Try it out, *Abba*. You have spent too much time lying here in this tent already," Jacob teased.

Isaac shook his head and laid the staff to the side.

Rebekah watched Jacob's countenance fall. She reached for him and rubbed his knee. "Perhaps later. Your *abba* is tired."

Jacob stood. He looked at his father's disfigured face before turning his pitied look on his mother.

Rebekah shrugged and motioned to the tent flap.

He bobbed his head and turned to leave.

She prepared a clean linen with honey and herbs as Hadiya had shown her and carefully wrapped it around Isaac's head.

When his face was behind the cloth again, Rebekah patted his hand. "Rest, my husband."

Chapter 12

*" '...and prepare for me delicious food, such as I love,
and bring it to me so that I may eat, that my soul may
bless you before I die.' "*
-Genesis 27:4

Beersheba, 1928 B.C.
Jacob

Jacob stoked the cooking fire. The cold weather had
pushed him home again making him restless. He
enjoyed spending time with his mother, but he would
rather be out in the wilderness with his flocks. His
father's shepherds had expanded to the point he spent
more time managing them than his own herd.

In the last thirteen harvests that he spent caring for
his father's flocks, Esau's wives had produced four
sons. In contrast, Jacob had not gone to fetch his
faraway bride nor taken a woman among the
Canaanites as he promised his mother. Seventy-seven

harvests had passed since he was laid on his mother's chest. When would it be his turn to be a father?

Since the day of his injury with Esau's wives' strange fire, Isaac had remained in his tent under the care of Rebekah. Esau had brought more and more choice meat to please Isaac's stomach and appease his own guilt. He was there again this morning. The two of them had bound themselves together with the fatness of the earth and pushed Jacob and his mother from their lives.

Each day had stolen a little more of the man's strength and senses. He barely left his sleeping mat and could scarcely function without help. He didn't acknowledge Jacob's hard work. The only thing that perked Isaac from his weakened state was when Esau returned from a successful hunt.

Jacob shook his head. It would not be long before Isaac joined his father. He was reaching the same age his brother Ishmael had been when he took his final breath. He tossed the stick into the flames and stood to flee to his family's altar to escape the eyes and ears of the tent city.

The stack of uncut stones stood waiting for its next sacrifice. In Isaac's condition, they had ceased offerings all together.

Jacob spread his hands over the stains and prayed, "Elohim, I know You hear. I know You see. Please show me Your path."

Footsteps alerted him to someone's approach

behind him. He turned to find his mother's flush face.

"Jacob, I'm so glad I found you."

"Is something wrong, *Ima*?"

"I just overheard your *abba* speaking with Esau." She took in a breath to steady herself. "He intends to bless him instead of you."

"But I purchased the birthright from my brother years ago."

"That may be true, but your father can still give Esau his blessing. He believes his days grow short. If he blesses your brother, then Esau will receive what rightfully belongs to you."

"You're sure of what you heard?"

"Your *abba* may be blind, but your *ima* has not grown deaf."

"What can we do?"

She paced around the stones. "There is no way on this brown earth that man is giving away everything you've worked for to that no-good brother of yours. It's Esau's fault your *abba* has no sight. You've taken his place and increased his flocks while your brother has wasted his days chasing game." She took a deep breath. "Melchizedek told me, 'Two nations are in your womb. The older will serve the younger.' It is Elohim's plan that you will rule over your brother."

"I agree." He spread his hands wide. "But what can be done? It is *abba's* right to bless whom he chooses." He watched his mother as unspoken thoughts swirled through her.

"I think I might have a way."

"What?"

"Go to the fields. Take two of the choice goats and kill them. Bring me the skins and prepare the meat as your *abba* likes." She stared deep into his eyes. "Don't let anyone see you or know what you're doing."

"Of course, *Ima*." Jacob hurried to the fields while he watched his mother move toward Esau's tent.

With a quick check, he picked two of the best goats and moved them to a secluded part of the field. He glanced around to make sure no one had seen him. Using his knife, he sliced the necks of both animals and he went to work removing their skin as best as he could and cleaning the meat from the bones.

Before long Jacob came to his mother's tent with arms full of fresh skin and choice meats. He added the hunks to the stew and handed the skins to Rebekah.

She pulled him into her private area of the tent she shared with Isaac. "Take off your clothes and put this on." She handed him Esau's tunic.

Jacob's nose wrinkled at the stench. "Why?"

"It's something I learned when I raised sheep."

He looked from the outstretched tunic in her hand to her face and back again.

"It's Esau's. His wives spend more time in the city than in his tent. I was able to sneak in to get it."

"But I'm still smooth and Esau is hairy." He rubbed his hairless arm. "One touch and *Abba* will know."

"That's what these are for." She held up her other arm with the fresh skins draped over it.

Jacob looked over the supplies of her plan. Images of sheep swam in his mind. "You mean to cover me in the hopes *Abba* will think me Esau? Like an ewe who lost a lamb?"

"Exactly. We cover you in Esau's tunic and some goat hair. Your father will think you're him and give you the blessing instead."

"And if I am discovered?"

"Esau will be gone for a while. By the time he returns, the blessing will be yours, and it won't matter."

He sighed and lifted his tunic over his head. With a quick movement, he pulled Esau's on. He lifted it from his body hoping the smell wouldn't seep into his skin. "The man has two wives, and neither one of them can clean his clothes?"

Rebekah pulled his arm. She wrapped the goatskin around his forearm and tied it in place with some thread. Motioning for the other, she repeated the process. "There."

Jacob looked down at his body. If his father could see, he would laugh him out of his tent. He ran his fingers through the wiry goat's hair. It was a perfect match to Esau's. He looked into the pleading eyes of his mother. "It might work."

"Stay here, I'll grab a bowl of stew." She hurried from the tent.

Jacob closed his eyes. *Elohim, I don't know what I'm walking into. I know You told my ima that I would be the one You favored. Help me, Elohim. Help me with my ima's plan.*

Rebekah returned. "Take this." She held out the bowl as if it held precious gems.

He reached for it. "What do I tell *Abba* if he asks why Esau...why I have come back so soon?"

Rebekah bit on her lip. "Tell him Elohim blessed you."

He nodded and took a deep breath. With a push of the dividing curtain, he disappeared to his father's side of the tent.

His focus remained on the stew as he walked until he got close to his father. He opened his mouth to speak, but closed it and coughed to clear his throat. Trying to deepen his voice to match his twin's, he said, "*Abba*, it is I."

"Esau?" Isaac sat up and searched through his darkness.

Jacob nodded, then remembered his father couldn't see. "I have done as you have asked and brought you stew from my wild meat. Eat and bless me."

"How have you come to bring it so quickly?"

"Elohim has blessed me."

Isaac tilted his head. "Come close so I can feel you."

Jacob moved slowly to set the bowl down and knelt

near his father.

Isaac reached out.

Reluctantly, Jacob moved his goat skin-covered arm toward his father.

Isaac's fingers ran over and over the hair as he drew deep breaths. He sat up and sniffed. "You sound like Jacob, but you feel like Esau." His hands went over the hair again. "Are you Esau?"

"I am."

Isaac eased back. "Bring me your dish so I may eat."

Jacob picked up the bowl and carefully placed it in his father's hands. He watched as Isaac drank down the stew.

Isaac held out the empty bowl. "Come near and kiss me, my son."

Jacob took the bowl and leaned near to kiss his father's cheeks. He heard his father take long slow breaths.

"You smell like Esau, like the wilderness of Elohim. Therefore, let Him give you of the dew of heaven, and the fatness of the earth, and plenty of corn and harvest. Let people serve you and nations bow down to you. Be master over your equals, and let your mother's son bow down to you. Cursed be every one that curses you, and blessed be any that bless you."

Jacob bowed. *There.* Isaac's blessing had been given. Nothing and no one could revoke it. He stood.

Rebekah caught his attention and motioned with her finger to come to her side of the tent.

She handed him his own tunic and turned so he could change.

He pulled the goat hair off his arms and replaced Esau's tunic with his own. With a flick, he tossed the disguising materials to the side.

Rebekah turned back and motioned quietly for them to step outside.

He nodded and made his way out.

She floated behind him.

"It's done, *Ima*. I got the blessing." He held out the empty bowl.

"Well done, my son, well done." She filled the bowl and handed it to him.

He received the stew, but his attention caught a form heading their way.

Esau had a bowl in his hand and a smug look on his face. He passed them without a word as he entered the tent.

Rebekah put a finger to her lips and pointed to the side of the tent.

Jacob followed her to the place she indicated. Through the goatskin, they could hear Isaac and Esau.

"*Abba*, I have returned with my savory stew," Esau boasted. "I have done as you requested, now bless me."

Stillness hung in the air like drying clothes.

Jacob looked at his mother.

She shrugged.

When Isaac's voice finally broke the silence, it was shaky, "Who are you?"

"*Abba*, it's me, Esau."

"Esau. You've already come and given me stew. Where is the man who came in before you? I ate his stew and gave him my blessing?"

Jacob heard a thud. No doubt it was the sound of the bowl of Esau's stew hitting the carpeted floor.

"*Abba*, have you no blessing left for me?"

Jacob could hear the despair in his brother's voice. His heart stung and his chest squeezed.

"Jacob..."

At the sound of his own name falling with hatred from his father's lips, Jacob nearly collapsed.

"...it must have been your brother who came in here dressed in deceit to steal your blessing."

"His name matches him well," Esau's voice fell in depth. "He has always been a deceiver. This is the second time he has stolen my rights away. *Abba*, have you nothing left to give me?"

"I have made your brother your master and given him the blessing of the fields. They will yield themselves to his hands. What more can I give you?"

"One small blessing," Esau pleaded. "You must have one small blessing left to give me."

"You will live off the fatness of the earth and of the dew. By your sword, you will live and will serve your brother. When you have dominion, you will break his yoke from off your neck."

Jacob met Rebekah's glance.

She reached out and held his hand.

The tent flap flew open. Esau spotted the two of them and rushed toward them.

Jacob moved Rebekah behind him.

Esau wagged his fat finger in Jacob's face nearly missing his nose. "You! I know what you did, *Jacob*," he spat his brother's name. "As soon as the days of mourning our father are over…" his eyebrows knitted together as he pressed his face within a breath of Jacob's, "… I will kill you."

Rebekah clung to Jacob's arm.

He held her back as he stared up at Esau.

Sweat pooled on Esau's upper lip as he sneered down on him, then turned to leave.

When Jacob was sure Esau was gone, he turned to pull his weeping mother into his arms. He stroked her hair as her tears wet his tunic. *What have we done, Elohim?*

Chapter 13

" 'Now therefore, my son, obey my voice. Arise, flee
to Laban my brother in Haran and stay with him a
while, until your brother's fury turns away...' "
-Genesis 27:43-44

Rebekah

Rebekah clung to her son. Her Jacob. What had she
done? Esau's words rang in her ears like thunder. *I will
kill you.*

She rubbed her damp face into Jacob's tunic. "I'm
so sorry. I never thought..." Sorrow coated her throat,
stealing her words.

"Shh." Jacob held her tight and brushed her hair.

She squeezed her eyes shut and prayed she could
take the day away. The ferocious look in Esau's eyes.
The fear in Jacob's he desperately tried to hide for her
sake. But the wild rhythm of his heartbeat and clammy
hands on her head revealed how truly shaken he must

be. What could be done to protect him?

Laban. The name seemed to drop into her mind like a water jar into a stream. She hadn't thought often of her distant brother and her relatives still living in Padanaram. *The girls.* Her nieces would be of marrying age and the betrothal offer on Jacob's behalf would still be in place even if Esau had declined his by taking other wives.

She jerked up to look into Jacob's eyes. "I have an idea."

A flash of concern struck across Jacob's face for a brief moment.

She couldn't blame him for his hesitation. Her last idea had been the catalyst for the threat now hanging around his neck. "Padanaram." The word spoken aloud sounded even more like hope in her ears.

"Where you're from?"

"Where my brother and his family still reside." Her heart raced ahead of the plan settling in her mind. "We send you there to fetch your bride."

"Like Eliezer did for you?"

Rebekah's heart squeezed at the name. Abraham's oldest and most trusted servant had come to live with them after his master's death. The servant had watched the boys grow into men, but had departed their life as gently as he entered it. They had mourned him many days, but his name still brought sweet sorrow to Rebekah's bones.

Jacob patted her arm. "*Ima?*"

She shook her head. "I'm well. I just miss him."

"Me too." He hugged her again and then released her.

"But yes, like Eliezer. I'll convince your *abba* to send you away to get your bride. I know Laban isn't the most honest man in the world, but with you there Esau won't follow. If he did, he'd have to officially break the betrothal and explain to Laban why he doesn't want his daughter. It's the perfect place of protection."

"But, *Ima*, I'm already seventy-seven, what young bride would want me?"

"Age doesn't matter in betrothal agreements." She waved off his apprehension like a bothersome fly. "If Laban hasn't broken his end of the agreement, then his daughter will still be unwed. Marry her and wait until I send word that Esau's wrath has cooled. Then you can return home."

"How are you going to convince *Abba*?"

"You leave that part to me." She patted his chest. "Whenever your *abba* calls for you, come to us and do whatever he says."

"Yes, *Ima*." He bowed.

"Good. Now, go check on the flocks and be ready to come."

"What about Esau? If he finds me, he—"

"Won't do anything until after your *abba's* death. You heard him. You're safe. But we don't know for how long."

Jacob turned from her and trotted off toward the

field.

Rebekah wiped her face and straightened the wrinkles from her dress. She took a deep breath and then set a scowl into place.

She made her way to the door of her tent and paused. *Give me words, Elohim.*

She pushed back the flap and entered. With exaggerated movements, she came to kneel beside Isaac.

"Rebekah?"

"It is I, my husband." She sighed louder than necessary.

"Are you ill?" Isaac groped in his personal darkness for her.

She reached her arm out so he could find her. "I detest my life because of the Hittite women."

Isaac tensed. "What have they done now?"

"They vex me. They've blinded you. My heart and soul ache with them near."

He eased back. "What can be done? They are Esau's wives."

"What of Jacob?"

Isaac sat up as if his son were standing before him ready to betray him again. "What of Jacob?"

"Don't you think it's time to send him for his bride? Please, husband," she lightened her voice to show submission, "if Jacob marries one of the Hittite women, my life will not be worth living."

He sat silently grinding the idea like barley heads.

"Send for Jacob."

Rebekah kissed Isaac's cheek and rushed away. She sent for Jacob to come quickly.

When Jacob entered, he immediately knelt in front of his father. "*Abba*, it is I, Jacob."

Rebekah would hear the tremble in his voice; she prayed Isaac could not.

"Now you wish to claim your true self?"

Isaac's words cut deep. Rebekah watched Jacob fold forward as his forehead almost touched the carpeted ground.

Isaac waited.

Rebekah wasn't sure for what; it seemed as if time stood still in their tent.

"I'm sending you to Padanaram," Isaac finally broke the silence. "Arise and go to the house of Bethuel, your mother's father, and take as your wife from there one of the daughters of Laban, your mother's brother."

Jacob moved to flee.

Isaac lifted a hand to place it on Jacob's head. "May Elohim bless you and make your fruitful that you may become a company of people." His fingers rubbed through Jacob's thick hair. "May He give the blessing of Abraham to you and to your offspring that you may take possession of the land that Elohim gave to Abraham."

Rebekah watched a tear trickle down Jacob's cheek.

"Thank you, *Abba*." He rose quietly and left the

tent.

Isaac's arm dropped to his side and his head fell with the movement.

Rebekah hoped he was praying. She lifted a few silent words to Elohim herself before leaving him alone.

Outside, Jacob was already pulling up the stakes of his simple tent.

She watched him for several moments until it felt as if her heart was breaking into a dozen channels like the Nile. Her reason for breathing was leaving. She would be stuck miles away not knowing if Jacob would honestly be safe from his brother's wrath.

He caught her gaze.

She tried to smile. Then a thought struck her. She dove back into her tent and retrieved a wrapped item. With it in hand, she made her way to Jacob.

His shoulders lifted at her approach.

"I was saving this for when you headed back to the wilderness, but I guess that's not going to happen now." She fought back tears and the rising lump in her throat. With shaking hands, she held out the gift.

He accepted it and set to unwrap it. Under the long piece of wool, he discovered a beautifully carved staff. He looked up at her.

"I spent the last several months making it for you." She smiled and traced some of her carvings. "I noticed you had outgrown your last one and it needed replacing."

"It's beautiful, *Ima*. Truly a precious gift."

She fell on his neck. "Jacob, I'm sorry. I never meant for any of this to happen."

He hugged her to himself. "Trust Elohim, *Ima*. Remember?"

She nodded against his shoulder. "I just wanted you to have a little piece of me to take with you."

He held her out. "I always have you with me."

She smiled up into his bright face. "May this staff be your strength until you return to me."

"May that be soon," he agreed, gripping the staff tight.

Rebekah stared at her son. How was she supposed to let him go? How long would she be required to keep him away until Esau's threat was gone? She didn't have any answers. The One Who Sees would have to be her eyes on her son.

The next several weeks were a blur of people and chores for Rebekah. She had seen Jacob off the same day she presented him with her staff along with one camel and a few packs filled as full as she could make them.

She stood on her toes watching his figure disappear over the horizon without even so much as a glance backward. She'd known it was for the best. If he saw her grief, he might have refused to leave. Even after his shape was gone from her sight, she still stood there, toes burning at her weight, neck stretched long as if she waited for him to turn right around anyway.

Her arms ached to hold him like when he was small. He fit perfectly in her arms until he outgrew them. Would she ever feel him in them again?

Warm tears raced down her cheeks as she returned to her cooking fire. She wiped them away.

Dust on the path kicked up and her heart leapt thinking Jacob had returned to her. When the man came into view, it was Esau. Her heart sank.

Behind him strolled a strange woman.

Something about her was familiar to Rebekah, but she couldn't place her.

The pair headed into Rebekah's tent.

She followed.

Esau knelt on one knee before his father and an arrogant grin painted on his face.

Rebekah's stomach turned glaring from him to the woman who stood straight as an arrow beside him.

"*Abba*," Esau bowed his head, even though his father couldn't see the movement, I want to introduce you to Mahalath, my new wife."

It took all Rebekah's strength to keep her feet rooted to the carpet instead of crossing the room and smacking the smug smile off her son's face.

Isaac sat gripping the wool blanket that lay across his lap. "Mahalath?"

"She's *Dod* Ishmael's daughter—"

"I know who she is."

Rebekah put a hand to her chest. The familiarity was now blinding. Mahalath held all the beauty of her grandmother Hagar combined perfectly with the strength of her father Ishmael. She was indeed a fine choice for any man. But Esau already had two wives.

"Her new name will be Bashemath," Esau explained.

The woman kept her gaze on the distant wall of the tent.

"Are you pleased, *Abba*?" Esau searched the empty gaze of Isaac. "I know you sent Jacob away to get a wife from among *Dod* Laban's daughters, I thought you would be more pleased with a choice from among your brother's."

Isaac reached out for his son.

Esau placed his head under his father's hand.

"May Elohim bless you and multiply you, my son."

Rebekah dug her fingernails into her palms. How could Isaac allow this? Would his preference of Esau know no boundaries?

She turned on her heels and fled the tent. Isaac probably didn't even know she had been there or cared for her opinion. He was blinded by more than strange fire; he was blinded by his own desires. She ached for Jacob and turned her anxious heart toward Elohim.

Chapter 14

*"And [Jacob] dreamed, and behold, there was a ladder
set up on the earth, and the top of it reached to
heaven. And behold, the angels of God were
ascending and descending on it!"*
-Genesis 28:12

Luz
Jacob

The camel under Jacob swayed with a steady gait. For
the countless time, he fought the urge to look over his
shoulder. His mother wouldn't be there; he just prayed
his brother wasn't either.

As the last part of the sun touched the horizon,
Jacob's eyelids began to fall. He hadn't taken the time
to stop since leaving Beersheba attempting to put as
much distance between himself and his brother as
possible. Now, the few days of travel had caught up
with him and his body needed rest.

With a simple tug on the camel's reins, he pulled him off the path into a clearing. He commanded the camel to kneel.

Jacob could feel the relief spread through the camel as well as himself. He dared a glimpse behind him. The path was empty. Only the stirring of wildlife and breeze surrounded him.

He took a deep breath and dismounted the beast. His fingers reached for the pack containing his tent, but he hesitated. What if Esau came upon him in the night? He pulled his hand back. No. He wouldn't even unpack the camel's load. If Esau came for him, he would be ready to flee in a moment.

He moved around the camel to stroke the animal's nose. "Sorry, Habibi. You'll have to sleep with those packs on for tonight."

The camel blinked at him with feather-like lashes.

Jacob looked around. The opening was not large, but it would do for one night's sleep. He had spent many nights laying under the stars watching over his flock. His chest tightened with the reminder of his vast collection of animals who were now without a shepherd. He hadn't even taken the time to speak with Jedidiah before leaving. What must he think of the runaway son?

He shook his head. His mother would see to his flock. A smile eased over his lips thinking of her. She'd probably take up a staff and tend them herself while he was away.

Away. The word sent a chill through his veins. How long would he have to be away from home?

He pulled his outer coat tighter around himself and looked around again. A small boulder lay nearby under a bare cedar tree. He commanded his camel to rise and led him toward it. "Guess this will do for a pillow tonight."

He secured the camel's lead to the trunk and settled on the rock.

The sky above darkened allowing the stars to peek out of the deep expanse.

Jacob tried to count them on nights he had to stay awake watching over the flocks. He drew pictures among them and played simple games in his mind to pass the time. Tonight didn't seem like a night for such ease. Esau's threat loomed over him. His father's death drew near. His mother was far away and would get further every day. He was heading to a place he'd never walked to meet the woman who would become his wife.

He sighed and closed his heavy eyes.

Jacob.

The sound, almost like a whisper on the wind, startled him. He looked up to see the vast night sky still hung overhead, but a distant light beckoned him. He rose and went to it.

In the middle of the clearing stood a massive ladder.

"Why hadn't I seen this before?" He moved closer

and looked up the ladder. Its top reached into the sky, past his view.

"Odd."

A man came near and ascended the ladder. But he wasn't like any man Jacob had ever seen before. His tunic was so white it almost gleaned like polished metal in the sun. The being's hair glinted as if it was dusted with gold flecks. On his back were two large wings forming what appeared to be a shield behind him. Though the feathers that resided there were not the soft fluff he had come to know from the many birds he encountered during his life. These were more like individual swords laying in rows overlapping each other.

He took a step back as another being, the first's equal, also ascended. Then one came down and walked among the field.

Jacob watched several beings climb up and down the strange ladder. He blinked several times trying to make the image before him make sense. What he concluded was that the scene before him did not belong in the world he knew.

As another stepped onto the first rung of the ladder, he paused. For the first time, one of the beings acknowledged him. The gaze was intense, but held no ill will. The non-man pointed up.

Jacob lifted his eyes to the highest point he could see.

A much larger being, who outshined the others was

above the ladder looking down.

"I am Elohim."

At the sound of His voice, Jacob's knees hit the dirt causing dust to fly around him. His body quaked as the words flooded him from the inside out.

"The God of Abraham. The God of Isaac. The land on which you lie will be given to you and your offspring. Your offspring will be like the dust of the earth."

As if controlled by the voice, particles of sand and dirt settled on Jacob's smooth arms.

He stared at the individual grains now covering him.

"You will spread abroad to the west, to the east, to the north, and to the south."

The wind kicked up picking the dust from his arms and carried it in several directions.

"Through you and your offspring all the families of the earth will be blessed. Behold, I am with you and will keep you wherever you go. I will bring you back to this land. I will not leave you until I have done what I have promised you."

Jacob dared to peek up, but a flash blinded him.

He blinked to find himself still laying with his head on the small boulder under the cedar tree. His camel lay next to him sound asleep. The stars shone above him. Everything was quiet.

He rose silently and moved to the middle of the field.

No ladder stood there. No beings ascended and descended. He looked up into the dark sky. No light shone down on him besides the moon.

"Surely, Elohim is in this place and I didn't know it."

He bent down and took a handful of sand into his palm. Allowing the grains to pass through his fingers, he watched as the wind carried some away.

"How wondrous is this place. This is none other than the house of Elohim and the gate to the abode of Elohim."

He returned to sleep, but with the early light of a new day, Jacob took the stone he had used for a pillow and moved it to the place he had seen the ladder. With a skin full of oil, he anointed the simple altar.

"This place will be called Bethel." He poured the oil over the rock. "If Elohim will be with me and will keep me in the way I go, and will give me bread to eat and clothing to wear, so I can come again to my *abba's* house in peace, then Elohim will be my God." He poured more oil out. "This stone, which I have set up as a pillar, will be Elohim's house." He looked up into the clear sky. "Of all that You give me, I will give the first part back to You."

Pleased with a fresh wash of Elohim's presence, Jacob mounted his camel and headed for Haran.

Chapter 15

"Now as soon as Jacob saw Rachel the daughter of Laban his mother's brother, and the sheep of Laban his mother's brother, Jacob came near and rolled the stone from the well's mouth and watered the flock of Laban his mother's brother."
-Genesis 29:10

Padanaram

Dust covered Jacob's hands and face. His throat was raw from thirst. It had been hours since his water skin yielded its last drops. The looming bright sun pounding down on him from above didn't help. If he didn't find water for himself and his camel soon, his brother would not need to hunt him.

In the distance, he saw a field with a small well sitting in the middle. He blinked several times praying it wasn't like Elohim's ladder and would disappear the moment he woke.

Pressing his camel, he came near enough to see three distinct flocks lying beside the well. The shepherds stood speaking to one another.

"Pardon me," Jacob bowed to them, "may I ask where you are from?"

One leaned on his staff. "We are from Haran."

I made it. "Do you know Laban?"

The silent conversation the three men had through their exchanged glances was not lost on Jacob. He feared he had said or done something wrong the way they hesitated at the sound of his uncle's name.

Finally, the first spoke again, "We know him."

"Is he well?"

The second clicked his tongue in a disapproving manner. "Oh, he is well." Then turned. "There is his daughter Rachel coming with her father's flocks."

A small figure appeared over the next ridge, leading the lankiest looking group of sheep Jacob had ever laid his eyes on. They looked as if they'd all drop dead in the grass before reaching the well.

Jacob turned back to the male shepherds and then looked up into the sky with a squint. "It is still high day and not time to bring in the flocks. Why don't you water your sheep and pasture them?"

"We can't." The first shrugged. "Not until all the flocks are gathered and the stone is rolled off the mouth of the well."

The small, distant figure came close to them. Rachel and her sheep gathered with the rest of the flocks.

Jacob turned to face her and it felt as if someone had reached into his chest and gripped his heart. His breath came in short spurts, and he feared he would never draw in another full one again.

Rachel was the most beautiful creature he had the privilege of laying his gaze on. She paused to untie her headwrap she had used to pin her hair up from the heat. The luscious flow of dusky hair fell down around her face and down her back. Its color and texture were a striking resemblance to his mother's.

Her dark eyes were framed perfectly with kohl, bringing all the attention to them. And the eyes themselves… Jacob felt he could get lost in the expanse of those eyes. Deep, dark pools like an oasis that reflected the clearest night sky he had ever seen.

His gaze traveled the rest of her features taking note of the lines of her lips and chin. When he reached her neck, he had to physically restrain himself from glancing further.

Rachel carefully re-tied her headwrap, creating a turban style to keep her hair away from her face.

Jacob heard snickering and sneering coming from the other shepherds. Their words of prodding and suggestion were not lost on his ears. He only hoped they saved that manner of talk for when Rachel wasn't around. None of them moved toward the well.

He wagged his head at them and stepped up to the well. His fingers gripped the smooth stone and with a few strong pushes he moved the cover off the well.

The mouths of the lazy shepherds hung open at him.

He had at least silenced their chatter. Grabbing the nearby water jar he lowered it into the well and drew water for Rachel's flock.

She sauntered toward him. The smile on her face brightened her eyes even more.

Jacob leaned down and kissed her cheeks. Her skin was as smooth as a freshly sheared lamb. A perfect combination of olive oil and myrrh scented her body and melted into the smell of fields and flocks. He breathed in her aroma trying to commit it to memory.

Tears stung at his eyes. He had never been so overwhelmed before. Not even when Esau threatened his life had he felt like weeping. But between the long journey, the heat of the day, the burn in his arms from moving such a large stone, and the beauty who stood before him, Jacob allowed the tears to flow.

"Forgive me." He bowed to Rachel. "I should introduce myself. My name is Jacob. I am one of your kinsmen. I'm Rebekah's son."

She squinted, studying his face.

Those night oasis eyes searched for truth among his words. Some type of realization struck her and she fled, leaving her flock behind.

The shepherds burst with laughter.

"Young man doesn't know how to handle a woman," the oldest joked.

"She ran like a frightened deer from a wolf," another cackled.

Jacob huffed at them and went back to watering Rachel's flock.

As soon as the other shepherds had their turn at the well, they departed. Jacob stood among Laban's flock alone thankful the others had heeded his advice to pasture their flocks elsewhere.

The sun hadn't moved far in the sky when another figure appeared over the ridge in the same direction Rachel had run. A large man hurried down the ridge and rushed into Jacob like a mighty wind. Massive arms surrounded him, squeezing the breath from his lungs. Rough lips covered by a shaggy beard kissed both his cheeks.

When he finally pulled away, Jacob could smell the distinct scent of old wine on the man's breath.

"Jacob! Jacob, my kinsmen!" Laban pulled him in for another round of greeting kisses before releasing him with a firm slap on the back. "Truly you are my bone and my flesh. You look much like Rebekah."

Jacob forced a smile while he rubbed his sore arms.

"Come! Come!" Laban turned and twisted Jacob to follow. "You must stay with me and tell me what news you have of my sister."

Jacob looked back over his shoulder. "What about your herds?"

Laban searched around. "The what?" He noticed the group of sheep laying by the well. "Oh, right.

Rachel is not far behind. She tends the flocks." He waved the concern off.

Jacob's feet tripped under the pull of Laban.

"Now, tell me, how is my sister?"

"She is well."

"Good. Good." He squeezed Jacob's arm. "And your father, Isaac, is he well?"

Jacob hesitated. "Not as well as he could be."

Laban sighed.

He had to hold his breath from the stench of rotting grapes.

"It seems we have much to speak on."

Jacob looked away. In his side vision, he caught Rachel returning. In the sunlight, she almost shined like one of Elohim's ladder-climbing beings. He wanted to rush back to her side, but Laban's grip on his arm wouldn't allow for a change in his steps.

Laban chattered on like a woman all the way to his home.

Over the last ridge, Jacob saw a group of several stone homes washed white. Laban led him down and toward one of the larger ones.

Women, young children, and servants moved everywhere. It reminded him of a stone version of his father's tent city.

"Leah," Laban called. "Fetch some water for our guest."

Jacob heard rustling nearby as he followed Laban into the main house.

Laban motioned to a stack of pillows. "Rest your feet."

He didn't have to give the offer twice. Jacob settled on the luxurious pillows, relief washing over his tired body.

A woman appeared in front of him, and he nearly jumped to his feet. He swallowed hard, forcing his body to stay in place. He slanted his head up at the woman. "Rachel?"

She smiled and extended a cup toward him.

"That's Leah," Laban explained. "Rachel's older twin sister."

Jacob stared at the woman. Her face was an exact match to her sister's. The lip and chin lines were drawn the same; their height and build were identical. If he had not seen Rachel heading toward the well, he would have thought she ran a secret path back to surprise them at the house.

His studying glare moved all over her face until he finally came to the woman's eyes. There. The only difference at all he could find in the two girls. Leah didn't paint kohl around her eyes, but that wasn't the only difference. Where Rachel's night oasis stood beckoning him to come swim, Leah's eyes were a deep void. *Nothingness.* It was the only way he could describe what he looked into. No light. No life. Nothingness. It was like looking into the blank stare of his father's damaged eyes. Leah's eyes didn't even brighten with her smile. A smile that started to fade the longer he stared at her.

"Forgive me." He shook his head as if trying to change the image in front of him. "I didn't mean to be impolite." He reached for the cup in her hand, taking care not to graze her fingers.

Leah bowed and left the room.

"So, Jacob, my boy," Laban sat on a nearby stack of pillows, "tell me of your family."

For the rest of the day, Jacob recounted all he could to his uncle. They spoke of family and land, people and possessions. Stories that had traveled far about Abraham's son and others that had not left the tent city he called home.

All the while, Leah made sure Jacob's cup stayed refilled with fresh water, and Laban never saw the bottom of his wine cup.

One day melted into a month for Jacob. The stay with his uncle felt like a blink of an eye. Each day he took it upon himself to rise before the sun and work the flocks near Rachel. Her presence was intoxicating. The more time he spent near her, the more he wanted to spend with her. The days in the field were never long enough and the nights were spent entertaining Laban with stories until Jacob couldn't keep his eyes open.

Upon returning to the house one evening, Laban met Jacob at the fold. He put an arm around the young man and walked with him to the house.

"You've been working my flocks for weeks now." Laban squeezed his shoulder.

Jacob glanced at Rachel as she counted the sheep for the night. "I have."

"Do you think because you are my relative that you should work for me for nothing?"

Jacob's heart slammed in his chest. "No! I-I-I," he grasped at words to explain that working the sheep was not only his passion, but that Laban's daughter had made the work feel more like play.

"Tell me then, what will your wages be?"

He scrunched his forehead. He'd only ever worked for his father. His flocks were his own. What would be a fair wage to work for another? Rachel's beautiful face came into his mind. "I'll work for you for seven years for your younger daughter Rachel."

Laban's feet faltered.

Jacob wasn't sure if it was his words or the number of wine cups his uncle had consumed through the day that caused the misstep.

With a tight squeeze, Laban hurried on. "It has been a long time that you've waited to claim her as your bride. It's not like I haven't had other offers." He sighed. "Abraham's servant came to Haran with multiple camels full of dowry for my sister's hand." He looked around. "You came here empty-handed."

Jacob couldn't deny the truth. The idea to fetch his bride had merely been a cover for hiding him among his uncle's household. It wasn't his intent to marry; not at his advanced age. His packs had only been filled with things he would need to survive the long journey. When he arrived, he had a few pieces of dried fruit, a camel, and a small tent. Nothing of any value to pay for the hand of such a beauty as Rachel.

"But it is better that I give her to you than I should give her to someone else." Laban paused and turned to Jacob. "Work for me seven years, and I will give you my daughter."

Jacob's chest felt as light as a feather. His toes lifted as if he would float away. Rachel would be his. It would cost him seven years of work, but if those could be spent by her side, he would gladly work every one of them with a smile on his face.

Chapter 16

"So Jacob served seven years for Rachel, and they seemed to him but a few days because of the love he had for her."
-Genesis 29:20

Padanaram, 1921 B.C.

Seven years had been a whisper on the wind to Jacob. Each day had met him with a bright sun and a warm smile from his betrothed as she waited for him so they could take the flocks out to the fields.

The time alone had given them opportunities to share about their lives and hopes for the future. By the end of his agreement, Jacob felt he knew his wife in every way except the one reserved for wedded pairs.

"A few more days, beloved," Jacob whispered in Rachel's ear while they reclined in the shade of their favorite acacia tree during high day.

She fed him pieces of goat cheese and fresh fruits.

The sound of her soft giggles sent chills down his

arms. Soon they would be as one. He was counting the moments.

Jacob looked out among their flock. Under his skilled hand, the sheep had multiplied in number and strength. Laban's herd now rivaled the neighboring shepherds' animals. His chest swelled with pride. Soon Rachel would be his bride, and they would return to his father's land and build a life together.

At week's end, Laban gathered people from all over to join in the wedding feast. Food and drink flowed through the night.

Even Jacob partook of wine at Laban's request. Though it was not his favorite drink and he rarely had the occasion to let his guard down as a shepherd, Jacob felt the need to celebrate his years of service that had finally come to an end and his prize who was waiting for him as soon as he could peel Laban off himself.

Laban called for Jacob's cup to be refilled as they sang and cheered well past sunset.

He put his hand over his cup, trying to save some of his senses to enjoy his first night with his bride. "Enough."

"Never!" Laban laughed. He pushed his hand away and refilled it himself. "Don't forget, my boy, you get an entire week to spend with your bride. You should relax more."

Jacob dipped the cup to his lips and drank the liquid in one mouthful.

Laban cheered and demanded another.

At some point in the lateness of the night, Jacob felt pressure on his arm. Laban was leading him somewhere. His mind felt as if a fog had rolled upon him without warning. He pressed his fingers into his forehead. "What's happening?"

"Your bride awaits," Laban's voice sounded odd and distant.

Rachel. The oasis eyes of his beloved swam in his mind's vision. He was finally being taken to claim her. Jacob yielded to Laban's leading.

Out in the field sat his small tent. Jacob had insisted on sleeping out there to protect the flock and remove any temptation to visit his bride in Laban's home before his service years ended. The family had agreed it would make the perfect marriage tent for the couple to share during their private week.

Laban stopped Jacob at the door of the tent. He put both hands on Jacob's arms and looked him right in the eyes. "Be kind to my daughter, son. She is inside waiting for you."

His uncle and now father-in-law's face swayed back and forth. Jacob couldn't focus. He gave a sharp nod, but instantly regretted the abrupt movement. The contents of his stomach threatened to reappear.

Laban turned him around and shoved him through the tent flap.

Jacob fell forward into the darkness, catching himself on a single woven carpet. No lamp was lit in the tent. He groped around.

A soft hand touched his.

The sensation that went from his hand up through his body was warm and inviting. He eased under the touch.

"Rachel," he whispered the name.

The soft hand wrapped around his.

He leaned forward searching for her.

In the dark of night, a goat skinned tent, and too much wine, Jacob yielded himself to the openness of the bride he had worked seven years for.

A bright light crashed onto Jacob's face. Daylight broke into his tent through the flapping door. The heat and intensity caused him to turn away. He groaned and covered his eyes. A pulsing pain beat in his brain. Why had he given in to Laban's insistence to drink so much? The smell of offerings wafted through the tent and turned his stomach. Who had left food out?

Just inside the tent flap was a tray of food. Someone must have slipped it in before he woke. The image of a woman's hand in his mind startled him. All of a sudden, the feeling that he was not alone in his tent set him on alert. Then he recalled last night had been the culmination of his betrothal agreement. He eased. Rachel had been fully his, and he didn't remember any of it. At least they had six more days to be together. No. Forever. They now had forever. Despite the agony in his head and the sickness that tore at his middle, he smiled.

Turning over again, he searched the small area for the body of his beloved.

She lay wrapped in a wool blanket huddled in a corner of the tent with her back to him.

With easy movements, Jacob crawled to her. He pushed some hair from her face, revealing the perfect lines he had fallen in love with. Leaning down, he brushed her exposed neck with soft kisses. "Awake, my beloved."

She stirred under him.

Holding his breath, he waited for her to open her eyes. He longed to look into those deep pools.

She rolled onto her back and eased her eyelids open with a flutter.

Jacob fell backward, scurrying away. The eyes. The eyes didn't belong to Rachel. They belonged to Leah. He rubbed the palms of his hands into his eyes trying to make sense of what must be a betrayal of his senses. He dared to look at her again.

Leah stared back at him with an empty glare.

"What are you doing in my tent?" He hurled the accusation at her while he fumbled around for something to cover his body. "Where is Rachel? What have you done with my bride?"

"I am your bride."

Her voice sent a cold blast through his veins. *No.* Jacob swallowed down the burn of acid that crawled up his throat. *It can't be.* Fighting to pull his tunic over his head, he hopped up and stormed out of the tent.

His bare feet stomped the worn path between his tent and the main house. Without a knock on the door or even an acknowledgment to the people who had risen to start the day, Jacob rushed past them all and right into Laban's bedchamber.

The man lay sprawled across his mat.

Jacob bent and lifted his father-in-law straight up into the air. His muscles burned with the movement. "On your feet!"

"What is the meaning of this?" Laban fought against his hold through an obvious lack of senses.

Jacob struggled to set the man on his feet. "What have you done to me? I served you for Rachel. Why have you deceived me?"

Shaking his head clear, Laban stared at Jacob. A grin of realization dawned on his face. "My son-in-law!"

Jacob tossed the man to the side not caring if his feet were steady enough to support his weight yet or not.

Laban faltered only slightly before righting himself. "Surely your mother explained how betrothals work in our country."

At the slight against his mother, Jacob gripped his fingers into fists at his sides. The man standing before him was about to taste his own blood if he didn't explain in a clear manner.

"We don't give the younger sister before the firstborn." Laban straightened his tousled tunic. "You arrived here before Esau. What was I supposed to do? Leah's betrothal needed to be complete before Rachel's."

Jacob's fury burned at his brother's name. The man's threats had sent him fleeing from his home. Now his absence had cost him his wife. "I don't have control over my brother's actions."

"I heard he already has three wives."

News of another marriage for Esau shocked Jacob for the briefest of moments. He wasn't surprised at the fact, just that Laban had received word before him.

"Ah," Laban pointed his thick finger in Jacob's face, "you knew Esau was already married and therefore had broken his betrothal with my daughter. Yet you neglected to inform me."

Smugness rolled off Laban in waves Jacob could almost taste. He wanted to wrestle this man to the ground and make him yield as Esau had done so many times to him. But as one deceiver looked on another, Jacob knew physical strength wasn't going to win this battle. "What do you suggest then?"

"At least complete the week of the firstborn, then I will give you the other."

Jacob raised an eyebrow. The man hadn't even taken a moment to think about the offer. Had he planned each step of this trap well before the wedding feast? Jacob folded his arms across his chest. He wasn't ready to trust this man again so quickly.

"If you work another seven years for her too."

There it was. The catch Jacob was waiting for. The wide, toothy grin on Laban's face was too much for Jacob. He was ready to turn and leave Haran, Laban, and Leah behind and run back to his mother. Then Rachel's form appeared in the doorway. Jacob's heart squeezed. He could see raw rope marks on her wrists and the way she kept her head down told him all he needed to know. She wasn't a willing participant in the deception. She had been just as much prey in Laban's trap as he. At that moment, he would do anything to free her from the grip of her cruel father. Even if it meant subjecting himself to another seven years of his service. Even if it meant he went home with two wives instead of one.

"Agreed," Jacob spoke through clenched teeth. "Seven years for Rachel."

"Seven years."

"For Rachel." He wanted it made clear. "Say it." Just in case Laban had any other women he wanted to try to tie around Jacob's neck.

Laban dipped his head slightly. "Seven years... for Rachel."

"And I only have to complete my week with Leah, then I can have Rachel as my wife."

"But Jacob, that's not how—"

Jacob took a step toward him. He felt heat rise into his face as his arms fell to his sides and his grip tightened.

Laban raised his hands, palms out, and took a step back. "Agreed. Agreed." He patted the air as if to push more space between them. "At the end of your bride week with Leah, I will prepare another feast and will give you Rachel."

Not giving Laban an opportunity to make any more bargains, Jacob turned on his heels and marched out of the room. He paused only a moment in front of Rachel. With outstretched fingers, he traced the marks on her wrists and then brushed away the tears from her cheeks. "One week will feel like a lifetime away from you."

More tears streaked down Rachel's face.

Jacob patted her arm. "One week." He glared at Laban before leaving the house.

The short path to his tent wasn't long enough to cool his wrath. He pulled the flap back and pressed into the tent.

Leah sat beside the tray of food. She jumped up at his return and bowed.

Jacob dropped to his knees on the carpet.

She settled slowly down. "Would you like something to eat?" She waved over the food. "My servant Zilpah prepared a wonderful offering for you."

"I'm not hungry."

"Oh." Her shoulders rolled forward and she set her hands in her lap.

Jacob looked at the face that closely mirrored his

distant love. How could he be so deceived? He sighed. Of course, he had deceived his father with a lot more trouble. A twin for a twin. The deceiver had been deceived. It was going to cost him another seven years from his home. What was his mother going to think when he returned with two wives?

After one week, Jacob stood in his second wedding feast staring at Rachel. He had refused every cup offered to him, even water. He was not giving Laban the chance to deceive him again.

When night had sufficiently fallen, he made his way to his father-in-law and demanded his bride.

"It is just now dark, what harm is it if you stay a little longer."

"Laban," the edge in Jacob's voice even raised the hair on the back of his own neck.

"As you wish." He led Jacob to the tent in the field and lifted the flap.

Jacob pressed in and saw Rachel sitting in the middle of his tent. His heart started to gallop. Seven years and one week. Time seemed to slow down around him as he reached his hand down to help her rise.

She placed her hand in his and stood to her feet.

He pulled her in close and allowed her unique scent of olive oil, myrrh, and fresh air to wash over him easing his tension. Nothing was going to take her away now. She would be his, and he would be hers. All of him. Though he had a first wife, no one could remove Rachel from the place she now resided in his heart. With all the gentleness he discovered in his strength, he opened himself to her and allowed her to open herself to him.

The next morning, Jacob awoke with a startle. Memories of the previous week came flooding back and his stomach sank. Would another woman lay in his tent? Images of his night with Rachel quickly overtook his fears. He rolled to see her smiling at him with those deep pools of bright eyes.

"My beloved," he whispered as he closed his eyes. "I am so glad to see you."

She giggled. "And I, you."

He pulled her close to himself. Her body molded perfectly into his as if they were two parts of the same form. This was how it should have been.

"Beloved?" her voice rose in question.

He rubbed his nose in her hair. "Yes?"

"Why didn't you put away my sister?"

The question caught him off guard. It was one he had struggled with himself over the past few days. "I didn't think it right. I'm sure it wasn't her fault, just like it wasn't yours."

Rachel tucked her head in closer. "You don't love her, do you?"

His heart ached for her. He had already worked seven years for Rachel and was getting ready to work seven more. What more could he do to prove his love for her?

Breathing in the quiet of the moment, Jacob had a thought. "Why doesn't Leah tend sheep with you?"

"She didn't tell you?"

Jacob shook his head. Though he had spent the past week alone with Leah, he had hardly spoken to her. They even slept on opposite sides of the tent.

"My sister is too tender-eyed toward living things." She rolled her eyes. "The first time *Abba* asked her to kill a snake she nearly fainted."

He chuckled.

"She was more than useless in the fields. She'd probably invite a wolf to eat freely from our flocks if it meant he didn't have to go hungry."

Jacob huffed. "She wouldn't have gotten along with Esau very well."

"Oh?"

"He's a hunter."

"Oh!" The idea brought amusement to her face. "Are you sure it's not too late to send her to him? I'm sure he'd like a fourth wife. She could be a gift."

Jacob let out a full belly laugh. He pushed some hair off her shoulder. "Oh, beloved you are cruel."

She pulled his face down and kissed him deeply.

Chapter 17

"My soul melts away for sorrow; strengthen me according to your word!"
-Psalm 119:28

Beersheba, 1916 B.C.
Rebekah

Rebekah's old bones protested her movement toward the cooking fire. Her bare feet shuffled in the sand because her back ached too much to bend over and tie on a pair of sandals.

She cringed when she saw Hadiya had beaten her to the fire. Again. The handmaid sat stirring the embers, awaking the flames to provide life for their small family. She shuffled on.

The servant smiled brightly, but her lips disappeared the moment she saw Rebekah. "Another rough night?"

Rebekah eased onto an overturned rock. Her body

was grateful for the rest. "You could say that."

Hadiya set a plate of simple offerings on Rebekah's lap and moved to grind some flour for bread. "I'll get the chores finished up. Why don't you eat something and then go lie back down?"

"What good would it do?" She popped a dried fig into her mouth. "Can't seem to sleep."

"What troubles you?" Hadiya's hands moved effortlessly with her tasks.

"Jacob." Simply saying her son's name brought fresh stabs of pain to her heart. "It's been twelve years since I saw his handsome face. I miss him."

Hadiya simply nodded.

Rebekah sighed at the rest of the food on her plate. She set it beside her feet and put her chin in her hands. "I miss him terribly."

"He will return to us one day."

"I don't know if Esau's wrath will ever cool toward his brother." She glanced over her shoulder in the direction of her tent. "Isaac assures me every day of his looming death. How can I call Jacob home when I don't know if he will ever be safe here?"

Hadiya reached a floured hand to her and covered Rebekah's knee. "We must find ways to move on, even with empty wells in our life." She patted her knee a few times and then returned to her grinding. "These people need you as their strong leader. We don't know how many more days Master Isaac has with us, but we should be grateful for each one."

"You're right." She set her eyes on the growing fire. "As always." Rebekah watched the movements of her handmaid. The rhythm of grinding and the contentment she displayed sent waves of peace over Rebekah. "Do you ever wish to be free?"

Hadiya's hands halted for a brief moment before returning to work. "I am already free."

Rebekah tilted her head at her handmaid. She couldn't remember a moment that she had given her a statement of freedom.

The woman set down her grinding stone and turned to look Rebekah in the eyes. "The day you purchased me from the slave stand, I've known nothing but kindness and love. But the day I took Master Isaac's God as my own, I've known a freedom no person can give or take away. My service to you comes from that freedom."

Rebekah's heart expanded. She'd always considered Hadiya as close as her nurse Deborah. Family. More than family. Much more like sisters than servants. She smiled at the thought.

Hadiya returned the smile and then continued her morning preparations.

Deborah came upon them with a jar of fresh water. She filled the larger jug that sat near the fire.

Rebekah grabbed her nurse's hand as she passed and gave it a gentle squeeze.

"Are you well, child?"

"I am now that you are here too."

The woman's gaze was curious. "You don't look well. Perhaps you should go back into the tent and get out of this heat."

Rebekah shook her head. "Isaac is still resting. Besides, I'd rather be out here helping." She stretched her fingers out as far as they would go. "These old hands can find some work to do." She chuckled.

Two figures approached from the distance.

Rebekah squinted. "Who does Jedidiah have with him?"

Both female servants looked up the path where her gaze led.

The lead shepherd guided a man toward them. "Mistress, Rebekah, this is Alhasan."

The stranger bowed to her.

"He comes from Haran with word about Jacob."

At the sound of her son's name, Rebekah rose to her feet. "Jacob?" Every joint in her body protested, but she didn't care.

"I have much news from your son."

"Please," she motioned with her hand, "sit and speak on while my handmaid prepares you some food."

The offer of a meal brought light to the man's face as he settled on a nearby stone. "That's very kind."

Jedidiah bowed and took his leave back to the fields.

Hadiya moved to add to the plate Rebekah had disregarded and set it between them.

Deborah ladled a cup of water and handed it to the

messenger.

Alhasan graciously accepted the drink and picked freely from the offerings.

Rebekah waited until he had seemed to have his fill. "Please, speak on."

"Your son Jacob is well."

The words were a balm to her soul. She could feel an unseen weight lift from her shoulders. "I'm glad to hear."

"He has wed and welcomed four children upon his lap. All sons. Reuben, Simeon, Levi, and Judah."

"Healthy?"

"Yes, Mistress. Very healthy, strong boys."

Rebekah breathed a sigh of relief. She turned to notice Deborah bow her head. They both knew that those sons should have been born in Deborah's arms, but Rebekah would see to that later. "What other news?"

"Another child is on the way."

"So soon?"

"Master Jacob's third wife is pregnant."

Third wife. The words turned Rebekah's stomach. A question plagued her as she stared into the face of the messenger. She knew she must ask, "H-h-how many wives does my son have?"

"Four."

Rebekah felt the world turn sideways and she gripped the sides of the rock under her for support. She feared falling forward into the flames.

Deborah appeared at her side with a cup of water. "Drink."

Rebekah took the cup and drank without thinking. She handed it back to Deborah. "Four?"

He nodded. "Though only one by his choosing."

The idea brought her little relief. "Would you be so kind as to start at the beginning of this tale and help me understand what has happened to my son?"

"You haven't received any other word?"

"You are the first messenger since Jacob left."

He rubbed his chin. "He's been with Master Laban's household for years. I thought he would have sent word by now…"

She waited.

"Forgive me," he shook his head, "I will start from what I know."

Deborah offered Rebekah another drink, but she waved her off.

"When Master Jacob came to Master Laban's house, he began working for him. It was over a month before they decided to set his wage. But Master Jacob only wanted one thing." He smiled. "Mistress Rachel."

"Laban's daughter?"

He gave a sharp nod. "His youngest daughter."

Rebekah rubbed her temple. "That was my doing. He was betrothed to her, and his brother to her older sister. Unfortunately, things didn't work out."

"Things didn't work out for Master Jacob either."

"Oh?"

"Master Laban tricked him on his wedding night. He switched Rachel for Leah."

"He what!" Rebekah jumped to her wobbly feet.

Hadiya came to her side. "Please, Rebekah, sit down."

Rebekah leaned around her. "My brother did what?"

"Mistress!" The handmaid pressed her to sit.

With reluctance, and a fire growing in her chest, she sat. "What happened?"

"Master Jacob had agreed to work for Master Laban for seven years. When the time was complete, during the night of the wedding feast, Laban took Rachel and bound her. He put Leah in Jacob's tent.

"The next morning when Jacob found Leah in his tent, he confronted Laban about it. Your brother revealed he knew about Esau's marriages and the broken betrothal and how it would mean endangering Leah's future if she didn't marry before Rachel."

"This is all my fault." Rebekah's head pounded. "I sent him into the wolf's den in an attempt to keep him from a viper." She kneaded her throbbing temples.

Alhasan hurried on, "When Mistress Rachel saw her sister continually give sons to Jacob while she remained childless, she forced him to take her handmaiden Bilhah so she could claim children through her. Bilhah is the one pregnant now. When Leah discovered this, she also gave Jacob her handmaid Zilpah so she could have more sons."

"I can't believe this." Rebekah rubbed her palms on her face. "I sent my son to Laban so he would be safe and now he's got more deception and trouble on his hands than if he would have stayed here."

Hadiya stepped forward. "You kept him alive."

"I sent him into a spider's web woven by my own brother's hand." She returned her gaze to the messenger. "I must send for him to return at once and remove him from my brother's grasp."

"You can't."

"Pardon me?"

"What I meant was that he can't leave yet. When Laban agreed to give Jacob Rachel too, they settled on another seven years of service. He is only halfway through fulfilling his dowry for her. He still has another three years left before he can leave Haran."

Rebekah's heart crushed inside her burning chest. More time away. More time in the hands of her brother. She turned her determined eyes on her nurse. "Deborah, you must go to him at once. It sounds as though Jacob has his hands full of wives and children."

"As you wish." Deborah pushed aside the tent flap and entered.

She turned back to the messenger. "You will see to her safety, yes?"

"With my life."

"She means a great deal to me, and my Jacob needs her." She rose. "Eat your fill and rest. When you are ready, Deborah will accompany you back to Haran."

179

She bowed and went into her tent.

Isaac still lay asleep on his mat. She'd have to wake him and relay the news she had been given. Deborah had one bag packed and was working on another.

Rebekah made her way to her side. "Bring him your strength, Deborah."

The older nurse looked up at her.

"And wait for word from me. I will make sure Esau is far away from here by the time Jacob's years of service are over so he can return to his home."

"What are you going to do?"

"Something." Rebekah shook her head. "Anything to get my Jacob back."

Chapter 18

" 'You know that I have served your father with all my
strength, yet your father has cheated me and changed
my wages ten times. But God did not permit him to
harm me.' "
-Genesis 31:6-7

Padanaram, 1908 B.C.
Jacob

Jacob rested under an acacia tree. The same tree he and
Rachel had sat under sharing their days together since
he came to Haran. Even after their marriage, he had
allowed her to continue shepherding with him until the
night she forced her handmaid on him. From that
moment on, he had sent her back to their group of
tents to deal with the collection of women and children
that were growing under his feet.

He rested his head back against the trunk. Life had
taken a path he never expected.

A few months of safe harbor had turned into

twenty years. After spending fourteen of those paying for his twin brides, he'd agreed to six more in order to build enough wealth to take them home. His wage agreement with Laban had since changed ten times and none in his favor.

A betrothal to one wife had turned into four marriages. Those four women had blessed him with eleven strong sons and one beautiful daughter.

Even the only wife that held his heart, Rachel, had held her own child. Their dear Joseph. He smiled thinking of them. Soon Rachel would add another. He smiled to himself. His beloved, his perfect oasis, was expanding with new life. Soon her child, their child, would be laid on his lap. A secret only the two of them shared for now. How he hoped it would be another son.

He sighed. As much joy as the thought brought him, his soul ached. That morning by the well, he overheard his brothers-in-law talking about him. They were blaming him for taking away what belonged to their father. Little did they know everything Jacob possessed had been given to him by Elohim, not Laban. The little Laban held in his hands was given away freely for wine and other fleshly gain. It was Laban's fault Laban was deprived, not Jacob's.

He closed his eyes and tried to breathe in the fresh air.

A voice called to him from a dream, "Jacob."

"Here I am!" Jacob called back.

"Lift up your eyes and see."

Jacob looked around. He was in the fields among his flocks. Sheep and goats of varying coat patterns mated and produced the like all around him.

"I have seen all that Laban is doing to you. I am the God of Bethel, where you anointed a pillar and made a vow to Me. Now arise, go out from this land and return to the land of your kinsmen. I will be with you."

Jacob awoke with a shake. The voice had breathed into him and awakened a fire inside his soul he didn't notice had been close to dying. He stood to his feet and looked out among his flock. His flock. It would have to be enough to leave. Elohim was telling him to go. He could feel the pull. Could hear the command ring in his ear like a melody that wouldn't leave. *Go.*

It was time to leave. His shoulders rolled forward. He would never be free of Laban's grasp. The man had done everything to keep Jacob tied to him like a senseless donkey. He would never agree to let him leave freely. An idea struck like lightning.

Hurrying, he found Alhasan tending further out. "Fetch Rachel and Leah and bring them to me here," he instructed. "But make sure no one from the household sees you."

"Right away." The servant fled.

Within moments, Rachel and Leah rushed to him. Rachel reached Jacob first. "What has happened?"

"I'm well." He pushed some hair back under her headwrap. "I need to speak to you and your sister...

privately." He took both of their hands and led them to sit under the acacia tree.

In hushed tones, he explained his plan to them, "I have seen your father's favor turn away from me, but the God of my father has been with me. You know I have served your father with all my strength, yet he has deceived me and changed my wages ten times. For that, Elohim has taken away the livestock of your father and given them to me." He took a breath. "I had a dream in which Elohim called to me. He told me to return home and that He would be with me."

"We know our father has done this and more," Rachel agreed. "He has even devoured the dowry you worked so hard for each of us and left us nothing."

"We have no inheritance in our father's house," Leah added. "All the riches Elohim has taken from our father should belong to us and our children."

Rachel beamed at him. "Whatever Elohim has told you to do, do it."

"Pack what you can in secret. Don't let anyone of your father's house know. Leave the tents for last. I will secure camels and we will flee tonight."

Seven days later, Jacob finally felt like he could let go of the breath he seemed to hold. He allowed the group to pitch a few tents in the mount of Gilead. They were not safe by any means, but with each night that came, he could feel the distance grow between him and his father-in-law's grip.

While the women prepared food, a snap of a branch in the distance brought Jacob to his feet with staff in hand.

"Peace," a familiar voice called out in the night.

Jacob didn't believe his hearing. "Come toward the firelight."

An older man appeared through the veil of darkness.

"Jedidiah?" Jacob rushed to the shepherd and fell on his neck. "What are you doing here?"

"Looking for you." He laughed and wrapped his arms around him. "I bring word from your mother."

Jacob pulled back. "Is she well?"

He smiled. "The last words she said to me were, 'Bring my son home or don't come home at all.' "

"That's my *ima*." Jacob slapped Jedidiah's arm. "You are looking well too, my friend."

"I keep busy running your father's flocks."

Jacob tensed. "Is he…"

Jedidiah put a hand on Jacob's shoulder. "Your father is the same since you left. Nothing has changed."

He could feel the tension leave his body.

"So, tell me," Jedidiah rubbed his hands by the fire, "what are you doing out here with your family. I thought I would find you in Padanaram."

Jacob swallowed hard. Thoughts of Laban stole his

peace. "We just left. Elohim called me home."

"And so has your mother." He chuckled.

"I can't wait to kiss her cheeks."

"No more than she. You are all she has spoken of since you left."

Jacob bowed his head. "That seems like so long ago."

Jedidiah's gaze wandered over the gathering. "It seems to be at least a lifetime ago."

Jacob looked to his family. "Forgive me. Allow me to introduce my wives and children."

"You mean my daughters and grandsons," Laban's voice boomed through the night.

Jacob nearly jumped out of his skin at the sound. He turned to brace for an attack.

"What have you done?" Laban emerged from the shadows shaking his head. "You have tricked me and driven away my daughters like captives of the sword?" He stood beside Rachel and held her by the shoulders.

Jacob could feel his blood boil at the way Laban squeezed her arms. He knew she wouldn't give her father the satisfaction of crying out. He tightened his grip on his staff.

"Why did you flee in secret? If you had only come to me and told me you were leaving, I would have sent you away with joy and singing." He moved to kiss Reuben's forehead. "Why didn't you permit me to kiss my grandsons and daughters farewell? Now, you have done foolishly." His head hung low as he shook it slowly. "It is in my power to harm you."

Jacob bit back the bile rising in his throat. He gripped his staff so tight, he feared snapping the thick wood in half. Let this old man try. He'd enjoy pinning him to the ground.

"But..." Laban moved among the group offering kisses and touches to those gathered, "...the god of your father spoke to me last night."

His father-in-law's words halted his thoughts. "Elohim?"

"That's the one." Laban put up a finger and waved it at Jacob. "He told me to be careful not to say anything to you, good or bad. And that you have left because you longed greatly for your father's house."

Jacob relaxed only a bit. "That's true."

He folded his arms across his chest. "Then why did you steal my gods?"

"I left because I was afraid that you would force your daughters to stay with you and not allow them to come with me. Search every possession. Anyone with whom you find your gods will not live." Jacob noticed Laban's sons and several men from Haran press in around them. "In the presence of our kinsmen, point out what I have taken that is yours and it will be returned to you."

Jacob stood with Jedidiah and his sons beside the fire as Laban and his sons searched through the few tents and several still packed bags for his gods. The sound of ruffling, emptying, and shoving grated in

Jacob's ears. Laban would truly not be satisfied until he turned over every rock in the mountain seeking his gods.

When he heard shouting coming from his own tent, he entered.

Rachel sat on her camel's saddle.

Laban stood over her demanding her to rise. His foot tapped an impatient rhythm.

"Don't be angry with me, *Abba*. I can't stand before you because the way of women is upon me."

Jacob's heart flipped. He worried what Rachel's words meant, but would not reveal their secret to her father. His anger reached past his lips, "What is my offense? What is my sin that you have pursued me? You have put your hand on all my goods; did you find your household gods? If so, then set them before our kinsmen."

Laban's face grew red.

"Twenty years I served you," Jacob continued, his voice rising with his fury. "Your ewes and female goats did not miscarry one time and I did not even eat of the rams of your flocks. Whatever was torn by wild beast, I bore the loss of.

"Twenty years. Fourteen for my wives, six for my flocks, yet you changed my wage ten times. If the God of my father, the God of Abraham, had not been on my side, surely you would have sent me away empty-handed. Elohim saw my affliction and labor of my hands and rebuked you last night."

Laban was quiet.

Too quiet for Jacob. Silence meant the old deceiver had time to think. To plan.

A sly smile spread across Laban's face. "These daughters are my daughters. These children are my children. The flocks and all that you see are mine."

Jacob waited. Whatever Laban was about to say next would reveal his true motive.

"What can I do this day for these my daughters and their children whom they have borne? Come," he put a hand on Jacob's arm and turned him to exit the tent, "let us make a covenant. You and I. Let it be a witness between the two of us."

A covenant. Jacob ran the words through his mind as he allowed Laban to guide him outside. His father-in-law wanted a covenant? It was unlike him. Or maybe it wasn't. A covenant would mean peace. Peace would mean his wealth wouldn't be in danger, at least from Jacob. Elohim must have sent some dream to the old man in order for Laban to seek a promise of peace.

They stood among the people.

Jacob turned to the men Laban had brought with him. "Gather stones." He shifted toward the women. "Prepare the food. We will eat by the pillar."

Bodies moved to obey Jacob's commands until a pile of uncut stones stood before him next to a large offering of food.

Jacob prayed and poured oil on the stones.

Laban ate and watched.

When all was complete, Jacob and Laban stood before the pillar.

"This place will be called Jegarsahadutha," Laban announced.

"We will call it Galeed," Jacob added.

"Galeed then. This heap is a witness between you and me today. Elohim will watch between us when we are out of one another's sight. If you oppress my daughters or take wives besides them, Elohim will be a witness to it even when we are apart."

Jacob raised an eyebrow. It was Laban who had tied two daughters around his neck instead of one and those two daughters had added two concubines. No matter what lay ahead of him, Jacob was sure he wasn't willingly going to add more wives.

"This heap," Laban continued, "is a witness. I will not pass over it to you and you will not pass over it to me to do harm."

Jacob imagined all the ways he'd like to bring harm to the head of his father-in-law, but allowed the images to pass. If there would truly be peace between them, as Laban was offering, he'd have to leave his hate on the altar along with his vow.

Laban waved his arms in the air. "The God of Abraham, the God of Nahor, the God of their father will judge between us."

Jacob nodded in agreement, but decided to add a clarification since Nahor and his father had called on many gods, "The God of Isaac will judge between us."

Chapter 19

"And the messengers returned to Jacob, saying, 'We came to your brother Esau, and he is coming to meet you, and there are four hundred men with him.' "
-Genesis 32:6

Mahanaim

Jacob and his family came to rest in a field to allow the flocks to graze.

As he stood watching the bounty before him, a being passed by he recognized. The shining face of one of Elohim's ladder-climbers walked beside him and toward the distance. Then another. And another. His body trembled as an entire army of them walked among his flock toward the direction they were headed. If they had carried swords, he would have fled to protect his people, but they merely walked among him.

Trembling knees hit the soft ground. His head fell

forward. "This is Elohim's host. I will call this place Mahanaim."

"Jacob!" Alhasan stirred him from his meditation.

He rose to see his messenger running toward him.

"What news have you?"

"It's your brother, Esau."

Jacob's chest squeezed. He had sent word of his request to meet and now the reply would be given.

"Your mother had sent him and his wives back to their land in Seir, that is why it took us so long to seek him."

"Did you give him my message?"

"Yes, Master Jacob. We told him that you wanted to speak with him."

"And?"

"He is coming..." the man fought for breath, "...he's coming with four hundred men."

Jacob's knees felt like shaking sands. Four hundred men were enough to kill every breathing thing under his protection. He had no warriors to fight for him. His sons, though old enough to marry, were only eleven in number. They could not defend the family. What was so few among so many?

"Any return word?"

Jacob put a hand on his messenger's shoulder, as much to steady himself as the man. "No. I want you to take Jedidiah and divide the camp into two bands. If Esau is coming with an army and they happen upon one company, the other can escape."

"As you wish." Alhasan hurried off to obey.

Jacob knelt, then laid face-first into the grass. "God of Abraham, God of my father Isaac, the One who told me to return to my country, I am not worthy of all the mercies and the truth that You have shown unto me. With my staff, I passed over this Jordan and now I have become two bands."

He reached out to grip his staff. "Deliver me from the hand of my brother. You promised to do good unto me and to make my seed as the sands."

He dug his fingers into the dirt under him. "Deliver me."

When he rose to his feet, Alhasan was returning.

"It has been done as you said."

"Well done." He patted the servant's arm. "Now, I want you and Jedidiah to walk among the flocks. We are going to prepare a gift for my brother. Two hundred she-goats, twenty male goats, two hundred ewes, and twenty rams. Thirty milking camels with their colts, forty cattle, and ten bulls. Twenty female donkeys and ten male donkeys."

"A grand offering."

"Let us hope it is enough." He turned the servant toward the herds. "Take them all and set them before the bands. When you meet Esau, and he asks about them, tell him they are a gift from his servant Jacob. Then have the two bands follow behind. I want you to drive everyone over the river tonight."

"What will you do, Master Jacob?"

"Stay here." He paused. "And pray. I will join you in the morning."

The faithful servant did as he was commanded.

By nightfall, all Jacob loved and cherished made camp on the other side of the Jordan. He sat alone on the empty side walking among the field.

When his legs could no longer carry his weight, he knelt in the stillness of the evening.

In the midst of praying, a force unlike anything Jacob had felt before knocked him to his face. Arms as thick as tree trunks wrapped around him like a snake.

On instinct from years of wrestling with Esau, Jacob moved into a defensive position. His leg came up to break the hold.

Legs, their arms' equals, tried to wrap Jacob's limbs, preventing him from escaping. The man spoke no words as the two struggled around on the ground.

Jacob's breathing became labored as he fought position for position to try to gain dominance over the man. In the darkened night, he could not see the man's features, and he moved too fast to catch a glimpse even in the dim light of the stars.

At many points during the long battle, Jacob thought of conceding. He had done so in every fight with Esau. That was the goal. Submission.

The man moved like a viper tying one of Jacob's legs with his own, pressing a knee into his groin.

Exhaustion tore through Jacob. *Not this night.* He wrapped one arm around the stranger's neck and the other he snaked under the man's arm and behind his head. Locking his wrists, Jacob fought to hold control. This night he would be the victor. For once in his life. If facing Esau in the coming days meant his death, then this last match would be claimed as a victory. One victory. It was all Jacob wanted.

With every joint and every fiber of every muscle screaming at him to cease, Jacob held his grasp as the darkness around them faded into morning's grey light.

With a delicate touch, the man reached down with his free hand and brushed Jacob's hip.

An intense burning in the hollow of Jacob's thigh sent his knee to the ground, giving the man enough leverage to almost pin him. Even through the pain, Jacob somehow managed to keep it from happening.

"Let me go," the man's voice was strong and steady as if he were resting instead of in the middle of hours of wrestling. "The day is breaking."

"I... will not... let you go... until... you... bless me," Jacob stammered through any air that would fill his lungs.

"What is your name?"

Sweat poured from Jacob's forehead. Burning through his body wore him down. The last time a man asked his name was his father the day he'd deceived him into giving him the blessing. He'd called himself Esau. He gritted his teeth. "Jacob."

"Your name will no longer be Jacob," the stranger's voice was robust. "Your name will be called

Israel because as a prince you have wrestled with God and with men and have prevailed."

Jacob pressed harder. "Tell me your name."

"Why do you ask my name when you already know it?"

Realization sent Jacob to his knees. The pain in his hip sent waves of agony through the rest of his body.

The stranger stood tall above him as the sun rose behind him, hiding his face. He put a hand on Jacob's head.

Words of blessing and peace washed fresh over Jacob. Tears stung his eyes as Elohim spoke over him.

When Jacob lifted his head, the man was gone. The peace left behind was tangible.

"Peniel," he spoke to the rising sun. "This place will be called Peniel because I have seen God face to face, and my life is intact."

He eased to his feet to stand, but his loose hip sent him back to his knees. The joint was so displaced he couldn't put weight on it. His gaze went over the area looking for assistance, but he remembered he had sent his entire family group across the river. Then he saw his staff laying in the sand where he left it. With slow movements, he half-crawled, half-dragged his leg toward it.

With his worn staff in hand, he pressed with all his strength to stand to his feet. It took a few times to find a rhythm enough to walk, but he managed to make it to the ford.

The water of the Jordan rushed by. Jacob sighed as he rubbed his hip. Even at this shallow point, how was he going to make it over the slippery rocks with a fresh and severe injury and no help?

With his staff as an aid, he took cautious steps through the stream. The sun completely cleared the horizon before he made it to the other side.

When he reached camp, Jedidiah met him. "Scouts spotted Esau."

Jacob saw the dust filling the distant horizon.

"He'll be here soon."

He put both hands on his staff and leaned his weight onto it. "Send the gifts."

The shepherd gathered the separated animals and set out.

Jacob sent his wives' handmaids with their children, then Leah with hers ahead. Finally, he held Rachel and Joseph back with him.

As they came within sight of Esau, Jacob bowed himself to the ground seven times. Each time sent new stabs of pain through his hip and leg. Each time more difficult to rise than the last.

By the time he had completed his sign of respect, the upper half of his tunic was drenched with sweat; the bottom still dripped with water from the Jordan. He put all his weight on the wood in his hand, praying to Elohim the staff would hold. He looked up to see Esau charging him.

No sword shone in his hand. No bow arched

toward him. Not even a sneer of anger touched Esau's lips.

Jacob hoped that no matter what form death would come from his brother's hand it would be as swift as Esau's feet.

His brother didn't stop when he reached Jacob. His arms encircled him and held him up until his feet left the ground. Wetness dripped onto Jacob's neck as he realized Esau was weeping.

When Esau set Jacob down, Jacob could not keep his own tears from flowing.

"Who are all these people you've sent ahead of you?"

Jacob wiped his face with his sleeve. "The children that Elohim has graciously given me." He waved to the women and children.

The gathering came near to them and bowed to Esau.

"What is the meaning of the herds driven before them?"

Jacob bowed his head. "They are a gift so that your servant might find grace in your sight."

"I have enough." Esau waved them off. "Keep what you have for yourself, Brother."

The word sent warm waves through Jacob fighting the chill of the morning air on his drenched clothes. In all their shared years, Esau had never used the term with such tenderness. He meant it. Jacob knew he did even if he didn't understand why.

"No. Please, if I have truly found grace in your eyes, then receive my gift. Elohim has been gracious to me; I want to bless you. I have enough."

Esau shrugged his massive shoulders. "If you insist."

Jacob watched the guard of four hundred men observe their interaction. "May I ask about them?" He motioned with his chin.

Esau smiled. "Merely a guard to escort my brother to Seir."

"Seir?"

"Why, yes. One can never be too careful on the journey." He wrapped a trunk of an arm around his brother. "You can live with me and raise your family under my protection."

Jacob weighed the offer. It sounded nice. To spend time with his brother. To live without fear. To expand his tents. But something pulled at him. "Brother, as you can see my flocks and children are with me. If your men should overdrive them, my flocks might die. Your men can move much quicker than we who have to give time for grazing and rest." He cleared his throat. "You go on ahead of us. I will lead my caravan as softly as they need until we meet with you in Seir."

"At least let me leave some of my guards with you."

"That won't be necessary." Jacob shook his hands, palms out. "You have been more than gracious. I beg you, really, let us have this pardon."

"If that is what you feel is best." He gave Jacob's

arm a quick squeeze and then stepped aside. "You do have a fine family, Brother."

Brother. The word tugged at Jacob. He knew he was deceiving Esau one last time, but he couldn't risk the lives of those who dwelt among his tents.

As he waved his brother off, he pointed his family to the west instead of the south. Their herds needed fresh grazing lands before heading home. Home was his aim and nothing was going to deter him.

Chapter 20

"Now Dinah the daughter of Leah, whom she had borne to Jacob, went out to see the women of the land."
-Genesis 34:1

Shechem

The air that blew around Jacob was noticeably warmer than the day before. He had spent the cold months lodging by any city that would welcome them in order to give his herds proper food and shelter. Finally, the weather was warming and that meant it would finally be time to head home.

Rachel ducked out of the tent to appear beside him.

Jacob smiled as he lifted a hand to her midsection. The secret they shared had grown too large to hide. In a few weeks, a new life would be added to their group.

"Are you joining the boys in the fields today?"

"Not today." He felt the babe inside her kick. "I

wanted to rest before we pack up."

"Truly?" Her eyes brightened.

His gaze met hers. "Truly."

"I will start packing right away." She turned to leave, but Jacob caught her arm.

"You do not have to rush." He pulled her under his arm and breathed in the scent that belonged only to Rachel. "There are plenty of hands around here to do the heavy lifting. I want you to stay well for our son."

"What if this baby is a girl?" Rachel rubbed her stomach. "Do you think Joseph would like a sister?"

"Knowing Joseph, he would love this child even if it came out a goat."

"Jacob!" She smacked his chest with the back of her hand. "Don't say such things."

He chuckled. "As much as I believe your child to be my twelfth son, if it is a girl, then she will be greatly loved. And of course, Joseph will love her. He is a constant guard to Leah's daughter Dinah. Those two have spent more time together than all the boys combined."

Rachel looked around. "Have you seen Dinah this morning?"

"I don't believe so." Jacob followed her glances. "Perhaps she is in her mother's tent."

"Perhaps." She shrugged. "I haven't seen her all morning, and she normally has returned from collecting water by this point in the day."

"Odd."

Leah came around the tent.

"Leah?" Jacob called her over.

"Yes?"

"Where is Dinah?"

She looked in the direction of the nearby city of Shechem. "Fetching water."

"But I sent her hours ago." Rachel glanced at the sky judging the position of the sun.

"You know that girl." Leah rolled her eyes and put a hand on her hip. "She is much more like you than I. She's probably abandoned her water pot to help the boys in the field."

"You know," Rachel tapped her finger to her cheek, "I did overhear her speaking with Bilhah last night about going into the city today for some festival for women."

Leah's cheeks flushed. "You don't think…"

"Oh, sister, forgive me." Rachel put her hand on Leah's arm. "I didn't mean to worry you. It's undoubtedly as you have said. She's probably with the boys."

"Jacob, please," Leah rushed to him and pulled at his arm, "let us go to the fields and check."

"Peace." He calmed her with a few strokes of her dark hair. "Wherever Dinah is, we will find her." He looked at Rachel. "You two stay here and keep an eye out for her in case she returns. I will go to the boys and seek her there."

"Thank you, Jacob." Leah bowed her head.

"Are you sure you wouldn't like some help?" Rachel offered.

His gaze went to her stomach. "Stay here and keep yourself safe. I will return with Dinah." Without another word, he hurried toward the fields.

The eleven boys were spread among the varying animals.

Joseph's form stood out with his brightly colored coat flapping in the wind. Rachel had made it for him with all the different wool they had acquired and recently surprised him with the gift.

Jacob went to him first. "Have you seen Dinah?"

"She went to the city this morning with her water pot." Joseph reached down to pet a speckled sheep. "I never saw her return."

"She's not in the tents, and her mother is worried."

Something dark settled over Joseph. "Do you think something has happened to her?"

"I'm not sure. She's never been gone this long, and the women are concerned for her wellbeing."

"Send me, *Abba*." He squared his shoulders. "I will go into the city and find her."

"Good boy." He patted his shoulder. "Go, and when you have found her, return to the tents."

Joseph's form disappeared over the horizon toward the city of Shechem.

Jacob found each of his other sons and hired hands to pass along the warning to keep an eye out for Dinah. They were to send her to her mother if they happened upon her. Then he returned to the tents.

Leah met him on the path. "Did you find her?"

"I sent Joseph into the city and the other shepherds are watching for her."

"Joseph is a good boy." She smiled a half-smile at Rachel as they neared the tents.

"Joseph?" Rachel rose from her seat.

Jacob waved her back down. "I was just letting Leah know that I sent Joseph into Shechem to look for Dinah. If anyone can find her, he will."

It was near nightfall when Joseph returned to the tent practically carrying Dinah.

Rachel and Leah rushed to her side.

"What happened to her?" Leah wiped her daughter's dusty face with the edge of her headwrap.

"She looks like she was attacked by a wild beast." Rachel brushed the girl's unruly hair searching for injuries.

"You can say that." The sternness in Joseph's voice stilled them all.

Jacob lifted an eyebrow. "Son?"

"I have much to say, *Abba*, but I don't think it needs to be repeated in Dinah's ear. She needs personal attention."

"Bring her into my tent." Leah moved to the side and pointed the way. "Rachel and I will see to her."

Joseph obeyed and set Dinah in her mother's tent before returning to his father's side.

"What happened to her?" Jacob demanded.

"Are the others in from the fields?"

"What does it matter?" He huffed. "Did one of them do this to her?"

"No." Joseph put his hands up. "But I think it best they hear this as well."

As they spoke, the other sons of Jacob approached. Joseph kept his gaze on his father.

"We missed you out there, Joseph." Reuben punched the younger man's shoulder. "Where did you run off to?"

Joseph stood stone still.

"Joseph?" Reuben looked between his brother and his father. "What's happened, *Abba*?"

"Gather, my sons. Joseph has something to tell us."

"Another dream again?" Levi joked.

"Silence," Jacob ordered. "Speak on, Joseph."

He took a deep breath, but his glare never left his father's face. "When *Abba* couldn't find Dinah, I offered to go into Shechem to search for her. I had seen her go to fetch water this morning." He took another breath. "I searched the entire city and finally found her."

"Is that all?" Simeon folded his arms across his chest. "You found a lost girl?"

Joseph set his firm eyes on his brother. "It was where I found her that bears weight on our family."

"Where?" Jacob demanded.

"In the palace."

"What was she doing there?" Reuben barked.

"During their festival, she had been mistaken as an available maiden. Prince Shechem, himself, had taken her and..." his voice faltered as he looked to his sandals.

"What, son?"

Joseph looked up into the eyes of his father. Tears streaked through the dirt on his cheeks. "He had defiled her. Had claimed her as his bride and was holding her captive in the palace. She was crying..." he swallowed hard and suppressed his own tears. "She was screaming a-a-and crying, begging for him to let her go so she could come home. She was shaking and could barely speak. I was only able to communicate with her on the way back through nods and shakes."

"Outrage!" Levi spit in the dirt.

"Savage!" Simeon balled his fists. "He can't do that to our sister."

Jacob pressed his hands toward them. "Peace, my sons."

"Peace?" Simeon scoffed. "These foreigners steal our sister and defile her and you call for peace? We should demand their blood!"

"We will give them a chance to make restitution for this offense."

Simeon shook his head. "I will only be satisfied with their heads brought to us on silver platters."

Some of the other sons cheered in agreement.

"I demand you to cease with this talk. No one will do anything to bring wrath upon this family. If you storm their gates demanding justice, they will snuff us out like a cooking fire." Jacob stood tall among his sons. "Allow me to handle this matter. For tonight, you all need to return to your own tents. I forbid any of you from setting one toe in Shechem. Do you understand?"

Reluctant nods and murmurs filled the air around them.

"Good." Jacob turned to Joseph. "Keep watch over Leah's tent tonight. Whatever they need, make sure it is provided for Dinah."

"As you wish." He moved toward the tent.

"Judah, you keep watch over the flocks tonight."

The man hurried back to the fields.

"The rest of you," he set eyes on Simeon and Levi, "I suggest you sleep. If your blood is too hot to do so, I suggest taking a cool dip in the river, but do not go near that city."

The boys turned their own directions, many still speaking in hushed tones about the situation left hanging for morning's light.

Jacob didn't have to worry about an audience with Prince Shechem and his father; the two men appeared at their camp as day broke.

Bilhah and Zilpah served food and drink to the guests while the other two wives remained in Leah's tent tending to Dinah.

Jacob watched the well-dressed and groomed men eat his offerings, drink his water, and sit among his fire. Half the boys remained to stand behind their father while the others went to relieve Judah in the fields.

Prince Shechem's father Hamor set his plate to the side and cleared his throat. "I'm sure by now you know why we have come, Jacob." He gestured to his son. "My son did not know your daughter was not of our city. She had joined in our festival and danced among our women."

"She is young and didn't know your customs," Jacob offered through gritted teeth.

"In the light of a new day, my son has seen his error and has come to make amends for the…" he waved his hand in the air searching for his next word, "…misunderstanding."

"Misunderstanding?" Levi nearly howled.

Jacob leaned over his shoulder. "Peace, son." He turned back to his guests. "And how exactly does your son intend to make things right?"

Prince Shechem stood. "I want to marry her."

"Sit." Hamor gripped his son's tunic and jerked him down.

The younger man pulled away. "I will not." He knelt before Jacob. "Good man, I need your daughter in my life. I won't be able to breathe without her near me. Since the moment my eyes saw her form, I have done nothing but think of her. My soul cries out for her." He crawled closer to Jacob, nearly pulling at his tunic. "Please. I must have her."

Hamor tugged his son back. "As you can see, my son greatly desires your daughter. Please. Let us form peace among our people so that your daughters can marry our sons, and your sons can marry our daughters."

Jacob heard his sons whisper behind him, but couldn't make out their words.

"Let me find grace in your sight," Prince Shechem begged. "Whatever you ask for her, I will give. Any dowry, anything at all, it will be yours. Just please say I may have her."

"You have defiled our sister," Simeon answered before Jacob could. "We cannot give her over to someone who treats her as such. Especially since you are uncircumcised."

Prince Shechem glanced over Jacob's shoulder to the brothers standing there like a city wall. "I'll do anything for her."

"Even be circumcised?" Levi asked.

"Anything."

More whispers.

It was Simeon who spoke for the group, "If you agree to all your men undergoing our circumcision, then we will be one people. But if you do not obey our command, then we will take our sister and leave."

"No, please." He stood and moved toward them. "We will do what you say. This night, all the men in Shechem will be circumcised."

Jacob glanced at Hamor.

"It will be done as you have said."

"Thank you." Prince Shechem kissed Jacob's cheeks and the tops of his hands. "Thank you."

Jacob waved him off. "Go. Do as you have said, and then I will give you my daughter."

The men left with joyous steps.

Jacob's sons return to the fields still speaking among themselves.

Jacob sat near his wives' cooking fire praying for Dinah and her bridegroom. He just hoped his daughter's marriage feast night would be happier than his own.

Three days later, Jacob stood with Leah and Rachel packing their tents. The men of Shechem had been true to their word. Jacob stood as witness to the circumcisions himself. He had given Dinah to her bridegroom. It wasn't how Jacob imagined he'd give away his only daughter, but at least the bridegroom seemed to love her. A life could be built on such.

As evening drew near, the distant sounds of shouts and screams tore through the air.

Jacob's attention shifted toward the city as he saw smoke begin to rise from behind the walls. His heart raced with thoughts of his sons in the fields. Would the unknown turmoil in Shechem reach its fingers of war toward his sons?

Joseph came over the ridge toward them. "*Abba* come quickly."

"What is it?"

"I tried to stop them. My brothers. They went into the city to get Dinah back and take revenge on Prince Shechem. Simeon and Levi took swords and when the others discovered their plan, they followed. Only Judah and I remained in the fields, and I have come to give you word."

"The men of the city outnumber them a great many; they have gone to their deaths."

"Don't you see, *Abba*? They planned it. All of it. They suggested circumcision not because they wanted to make peace with Shechem, but because it would weaken their men."

"They plan on slaughtering an entire city to cool their wrath?"

Joseph grew pale.

Jacob turned at the sound of approaching feet.

Over the ridge, Simeon and Levi led a group of their brothers along with a band of numerous women, children, and animals.

Jacob's stomach turned at the sight of his sons. They held swords at their sides still dripping with the blood of the relatives of the people they led toward him. In the distance, the smoke from the city rose higher into the air. Worst of all, the two leaders' faces held pride. Pure pride. They were pleased with their actions.

When they came within speaking distance, Jacob could see Dinah's form behind her two brothers. She looked so small and brittle standing behind the wall of arrogance. She had been ripped away from them, defiled, purchased, and now ripped away again. The woman looked as if the next strong breeze would shatter her into pieces.

"What is the meaning of this display?" Jacob snapped.

"We have restored our sister," Levi offered. "When you would not."

"What are you talking about? Prince Shechem paid Dinah's dowry, and the men of the city did all that you asked. They paid for his mistake with their blood."

"Now they have!" Simeon held his sword high. "A few drops were not enough. We have spilled it all as payment for our sister's defilement."

"All?" Jacob swallowed as he looked into the downward cast eyes of the women and children who stood silent.

"All," Simeon clarified. "Prince Shechem, his father, and every male we could find. Our swords have tasted Shechem's blood this day and now our sister is cleansed."

"And what of your sister?" He motioned toward her. "She was a wife and now what? She cannot marry anyone now that you have slain her bridegroom."

"We have slain her defiler," Levi barked. "She is

cleansed and free to marry from our own tribe."

"My sons." Jacob hung his head. "What have you done?" He looked up at them. "This abomination will cause us to be a stench in the nostrils of the surrounding people. They will gather themselves together against us to slay us."

"What were we supposed to do?" Simeon stepped forward, challenging his father. "Should we have just allowed that foreigner to deal with our sister as if she were some harlot?" He didn't wait for his father's answer, but pressed past him and motioned for the others to follow.

Jacob watched the large band of new widows and orphans march behind him in silence. Spoils of war. Elohim had promised his people would be more than the sands, but he didn't think He meant like this.

That night, Jacob tossed upon his mat. Visions of blood and widows' screams kept sleep at bay.

Before morning broke, Elohim's voice ripped through the nightmares, "Rise. Go to Bethel. Make an altar to me where I appeared to you when you fled from Esau's face."

Jacob sat up. Elohim's call echoed in his mind. *Go.*

At sunrise, he gathered the people together by a large oak. He spoke to them of Elohim and the land of his father. He offered them protection and peace but required only one thing. They each had to remove any objects they had in their possessions that were given over to their gods. He had already stared down death from Laban for being accused of stealing gods, it would not be a mistake he made again.

While his boys dug a large pit near the tree, the people came to drop their statues, earrings, nose rings, and pendants into the hole.

Rachel stepped forward and he scrunched his forehead at her. She dropped a wrapped package into the pit and turned away.

Her father's gods. The idea slashed at his insides. She must have been the one who took them. It explained why she lied to her father when he came hunting for them.

He hung his head. At least she was giving them up now. His heart galloped up into his throat as he watched her form move back to the tents. That day in the mountain, he had called a curse of death upon the one found with them. She had not been discovered with the stolen goods. Did that mean she would be spared?

He shuddered. Their child still kicked in her stomach. Would Jacob get to hold his son and still see days with the wife of his heart? Would Elohim spare the love of his soul for her choice? He had forgiven Jacob so many times. Did He have one more pardon left?

Chapter 21

*" 'There is hope for your future,' declares the LORD,
'and your children shall come back to their own
country.' "
-Jeremiah 31:17*

Beersheba
Rebekah

Rebekah watched the endless energy that was the children of her tent city. As the guard dogs followed them, she kept her eyes on them as well. With all the help a woman could ask for, there wasn't much left for her old body to do.

Each task she attempted took longer and longer to complete. Her fingers weren't as nimble as she remembered. Her back ached far earlier in the day than she wanted. Even her breathing became a challenge if she tried to keep up with the younger women.

She leaned back allowing the sun to shine down on

her. At least she was alive. At least she could enjoy those she shared life with.

"Feeling better today?"

Rebekah didn't have to open her eyes to know the question came from the lips of her handmaid, Hadiya. She was probably busying herself with some chore that Rebekah should be doing. "Well enough." She opened her eyes. She was right.

Hadiya had a basket of freshly washed garments on her hip. "Can I help you inside the tent? I can raise a side or two to let in the breeze."

"I'd rather sit out here and drink in Elohim's day for a few more moments."

"As you wish." She sat beside her and sifted through the garments to check for holes that needed mending.

The two women sat in silence; content with each other's presence.

Rebekah sighed.

"Something I can do for you?"

"There is only one thing my soul desires."

"Jacob?"

"Jacob."

Hadiya shook her head.

"It's been far too long. I sent Jedidiah months ago. They should have returned by now."

Hadiya poked her finger through a worn place in one of Isaac's tunics. "You know how travel is. If he was driving herds they probably stopped to winter somewhere."

"I suppose." She reached over to finger the tunic. "Could I try mending that one?"

Hadiya raised an eyebrow at her. "It will take me no time to fix it."

"I know." She dropped the material. "It's just that I feel so useless these days."

"You entertain the children with stories."

"Yes, but most of them can't sit still long enough for me to finish one."

She chuckled.

"Besides, I want to see the faces of my grandsons. They are all probably grown with children of their own by now."

"Wouldn't that be something?"

She sighed again. "It would have been nice to set one of Jacob's children upon my lap."

"There is still time."

"Still, I would settle for one of his grandchildren."

One of the shepherds drew near to them. "Pardon me, Mistress Rebekah."

"Tobiah, speak on, dear one."

He bowed. "I have a man who came upon us in the fields who says he has a message for you."

"Bring him to me."

Tobiah bowed and returned with a man Rebekah hadn't laid eyes on in years.

"Alhasan?"

The shepherd bowed low. "I am he, Mistress."

"You carry word from Jacob?"

"I do."

"Speak on then before these old bones turn to dust while you stand there holding your tongue."

Hadiya shook her head.

He smiled at her. "Your son is in Bethel and calls for you and Isaac to come to him."

"Jacob? So near." Tears stung her dry eyes. "He calls for me?"

"I can be ready to guide you as soon as you're ready."

Rebekah rose on shaky legs. "I must tell Isaac." She hurried as fast as her feet could shuffle into her tent. "Husband, I have word from our son."

Isaac sat up. "Esau?"

"Jacob. He is in Bethel and calls for us."

"Oh." Isaac eased back down. "I'm sorry, beloved. I don't think I am strong enough for such a journey."

"But, husband," she moved to kneel beside him, "you've laid upon that mat for over twenty years claiming each day would be your last. Please. Rise and come with me to see how Elohim has blessed our son."

He shook his head and turned over onto his side.

Rebekah huffed at him. If Isaac wasn't willing to go, she didn't need him. She rose and left the tent. She knew at least Hadiya would accompany her and Alhasan. Her prayers would finally come true. Jacob. Her Jacob. She would see her son's face in a matter of days.

Chapter 22

"And Jacob set up a pillar in the place where he had spoken with him, a pillar of stone. He poured out a drink offering on it and poured oil on it. So Jacob called the name of the place where God had spoken with him Bethel."
-Genesis 35:14-15

Bethel

Rebekah was afraid to blink as she stared down the path. She stood beside the small boulder waiting for signs of Jacob's caravan. The air around her was calm and the field was empty except for her, Alhasan, and Hadiya.

The woman who had seen most of life with her stood as beautiful as any statue man could carve. Her grey hair matched Rebekah's, as did the wide and anticipating smile spread across her face.

Rebekah's heart raced as she lifted a hand to shield

her eyes from the bright sun.

Finally, in the distance to the north, a form appeared leading a band so vast Rebekah couldn't see where it ended. People and animals walked at a steady pace. In front, was a lone figure whose gait was slow, but so familiar Rebekah couldn't mistake it for another. Jacob had left home empty-handed, but was returning with a caravan that rivaled the size of Abraham's.

"Jacob." His name tasted so sweet on her tongue it was as if she had bitten into a honeycomb. Her toes tingled in her sandals as she thought about running toward him. At her advanced age, it was probably not the best idea.

Jedidiah walked only a pace behind with Deborah beside him.

That shepherd is getting an extra serving of stew tonight for bringing my Jacob home. Rebekah's entire body warmed as they drew near.

With only a stone's throw distance between them, Rebekah noticed Jacob leaning heavily on his staff. Her smile reached up to her ears. The familiar carvings were worn, but still there. After twenty years, he held tight to the staff she had given him the last time they saw each other.

Tears blurred her vision, and she wiped them away quickly so as not to lose sight of her son. He seemed as worn as his staff. He walked with a noticeable limp and her heart ached to know what life had heaved upon him. Whatever it was, a bright grin illuminated his entire face. He was at peace. She had never seen a man so calm. His face almost outshined the sun that beat down on them. Perhaps whatever caused him to lean upon his staff had not been such a terrible thing.

He walked right up to her and smiled. "Hello, *Ima*."

Rebekah fell onto his neck, weeping. "Jacob, my Jacob. You're home." She breathed in his familiar scent, never wanting to let him go again.

He bent to look into her face. "Call me Israel."

She squinted at him. The peace in his eyes intensified to the point she almost couldn't hold his gaze. "Israel?"

His smile broadened.

Behind the grin, she could tell there was a story she needed to hear. Esau had become a prince among men. Now, her Jacob had become *Israel, a prince with God.* "I like it." She beamed. "It suits you."

He moved to wave behind him. "*Ima*, I'd like to introduce you to my wives."

At the words, Rebekah's heart sank. Her precious son, Jacob… Israel… had followed in his brother's steps instead of his father's and taken more than one wife. She had been warned, but to see them standing behind him now made it too real. She swallowed hard and tried to keep the smile on her lips.

"This is Rachel." Israel put an arm around the slender shoulders of a heavily pregnant woman. His hand protectively covered her middle.

The Hope

Rebekah looked at the beautiful face of her niece. Her bright eyes shone and her skin glowed with vigor only experienced by a woman carrying new life. The deep, dark strands of her luscious hair were a perfect match to the hair of her youth. She could see how this woman had stolen her son's heart. "It's a pleasure to meet you, Rachel. When are you expecting?"

"Any day now." She put her hand on top of her husband's and grinned.

Rebekah fought the urge to scold her son. How could he travel with a woman so close to delivering? Though it was her word that had sent for him to come home.

"And this," Israel waved his staff, "is her sister Leah."

A woman almost matching Rachel stepped forward and bowed.

The resemblance between them was undeniable. The two women could be one and the same if one didn't look close enough. The more Rebekah's stared, the more she saw the slight differences. Leah seemed to carry herself much more humbly. Her gaze didn't penetrate Rebekah as Rachel's had. Leah appeared softer and quieter as if she believed even if she happened to breathe too hard it might cause damage. Rachel lifted her chin and met everyone's glare. It was as if she could stare down anything that came against her.

"These are my other two wives, Bilhah and

Zilpah."

Two women stood behind Leah; both bowed respectfully to Rebekah.

She looked into her son's face and raised an eyebrow.

He chuckled. "We have much to speak about."

"Yes, we do." She raised her eyebrow higher. "We certainly do."

Israel cleared his throat and removed his arm from around Rachel. "And these are my children."

A group of people stepped closer. Most of them far from being considered children.

"Reuben, Simeon, Levi, Judah, Issachar, Zebulun, Dan, Naphtali, Gad, Asher, Dinah…"

Each bowed in turn as their father called their name.

"…and this is Joseph."

The young man stood among his older siblings. His thick hair matched his mother's and his face mirrored his father's. A coat woven with bright colors whipped around him in the wind.

Rebekah caught a look in her son's eyes she had seen too many times before. This was his favored son. By Joseph's stature and the bit of roundness still left in his face from childhood, she could tell he was the youngest of the group. Her heart squeezed. Would Israel follow too closely in his father's faulty footsteps? She had many questions for whenever she could get a few moments with him away from the rest.

Israel's gaze fell on her. "You look well, *Ima*."

"I am, my son." She smiled. "But no matter how many days Elohim gives me, I'm ready to see the One Who Sees me."

He beamed, but a sudden wave of concern washed over him. "And *Abba*?"

"Still pesters me daily to make him Esau's stew."

He laughed.

Rebekah's chest tightened. "Have you seen your brother?"

"We have made peace."

She breathed a sigh of relief. Twenty years of grief, mourning, and worry lifted off her shoulders with the simple word. "I am so very glad to hear that."

"We have much to speak on," he reached to take her hand, "but I must first confirm my oath with Elohim." He squeezed her hand and then moved past her toward the boulder.

Israel's four wives followed closely behind as if they were camels on leads.

The rest of the gathering stood on the path watching their patriarch.

When Rebekah turned to move, her foot slipped on a rock. A hand came under her elbow to steady her. She looked up into the smiling face of Joseph.

"May I assist you, Great *Ima* Rebekah?"

"Thank you." She leaned into his strength as they walked.

"*Abba* tells me you used to have dreams of

Elohim."

Rebekah glanced in Israel's direction, but he was too far away to hear their conversation. "Did he?"

The young man nodded vigorously.

"And why would he share such information with you?"

"Because I do, too."

Rebekah halted. She stared into his deep gaze. "You do?"

"I've had many dreams." He looked around, leaned closer, and whispered, "Sometimes Elohim even speaks to me in them."

A warming sensation filled her on the inside. "You keep listening to that voice, Joseph. Elohim will guide you."

He nodded and turned them toward the pillar.

Rebekah watched as Israel took a skin full of oil from his side and poured it over the rock. With lifted hands, he prayed to the God they shared.

As she looked on the son who was loved by Elohim, her thoughts drifted to the one far away. The brothers had made peace. She had made peace within her soul over her distant son. Though Esau was hated by Elohim, she still cared for him. If Elohim had reached her, what stopped Him from reaching Esau? Even if Elohim called to Esau as He had in her dreams, would the man choose to listen?

Her heart lifted at the idea that one day Esau might call on the One Who Sees too, but she finally understood she could never force anyone. Each person had to make the choice for themselves. Just as Abraham had, just as Isaac had, just as Jacob had... just as she had. She would choose to continue to pray for Esau and hold onto hope.

What To Read Next?

Jesus changed millions of lives; his was one of the first.

After conflict and betrayal result in the arrest of Jesus, James is forced to turn his back on his brother.

Sentenced to death by crucifixion, Jerusalem is painted with his brother's blood. James' mourning is met with fear when whispers of Jesus' resurrection fill the streets.

Obligated to take charge of a divided family, James must protect his siblings from blood-thirsty Rome and a pious council until they can flee the riotous city.

Will they endure the same fate as their oldest brother?

If you want to experience the sights, smells, and sounds of first-century Jerusalem in the wake of Jesus' resurrection, then you don't want to miss this series. *James* is book one in the Servant Siblings series.

Also by Jenifer Jennings:

Special Collections and Boxed Sets
Biblical Historical stories from the Old Testament to the New, these special boxed editions offer a great way to catch up or to fall in love with Jenifer Jennings' books for the first time.

Faith Finder Series: Books 1-3
Faith Finders Series: Books 4-6
The Rebekah Series: Books 1-3

* * *

Faith Finders Series:
Go deeper into the stories of these familiar faith heroines.

Midwives of Moses
Wilderness Wanderer
Crimson Cord
A Stolen Wife
At His Feet
Lasting Legacy

* * *

The Rebekah Series:
Follow Rebekah on her faith journey from the fields of her homeland to being part of Abraham's family.

The Stranger
The Journey
The Hope

* * *

Servant Siblings Series:
They were Jesus' siblings, but they become His followers.

James
Joseph
Assia
Jude
Lydia
Simon
Salome

Find all of these titles at your favorite retailer or at:
jeniferjennings.com/books

Thank You!

Hubby, without your hard work and constant support none of my words would reach readers. Thank you for always having my "six" and being my shoulders to lean on.

Kids, through this season of our world being turned upside down we still held tight to each other. Though I never planned to release these stories while we hunkered at home, your patience and understanding helped push me to finish.

Clay County Word Weavers, once again you women have proven your worth far more than gold. Knowing I had a safe place to unveil the first tries of this story made me anticipate meeting with you every month. Thank you for graciously improving each story I offer.

Jill, my editor, or the title I much more prefer- Typo Huntress, your willingness to work with me among your own life is always a God-send. Your fresh eyes and eager anticipation to get lost in my books drive me to race towards the end. These works would not be what they are today without you.

Jenifer's Jewels, you are more than my ARC team - you are the readers I enjoy hearing from most. Your foundational support paves the path for the reviews from others. I long to finish each book so I can hear your responses first. Thank you for being the first to hunger for them.

Reader, though you're usually not the first to read

my books, I certainly think of you first when writing them. I imagine what you do while you dive deep into these stories. I picture God reaching down into your life through my words and cradling your heart and soul in his hands. Cling tight to Jesus, beloved, He is worth it.

About the Author

Jenifer Jennings writes Christian Fiction to inspire her readers in their next step of faith with God. It's no surprise that her favorite verse is Hebrews 11:6.

She earned a Bachelor's degree in Women's Ministry from Trinity Baptist College and a Master's in Biblical Languages from Liberty University. She is also a member of Word Weavers International.

Jenifer uses her writing to grow closer to her Lord. Her deepest desire is that, through her work, God would bring others into a deeper relationship with Himself.

Between studying and writing, she is a dedicated wife, loving mother of two children, and lives in North Florida.

If you'd like to keep up with new releases, receive spiritual encouragement, and get your hands on a FREE book, then join Jenifer's Newsletter: jeniferjennings.com/gift